**"Tessa, we have to get out of here,"
Brax whispered.**

"What are we going to do?" Tessa's eyes widened with terror.

"Go out the back. There's someone waiting in front. Keep Walker as quiet as you can and follow me. Don't say a word."

Even though everything looked quiet behind the house, Brax constantly scanned the area and listened hard. He took Tessa's arm and led her away as he continued to survey the grounds. Every crunch, every footstep rang out like a gong.

He wasn't surprised when he heard a heavy tread coming their way from the side of the house. Brax pushed Tessa toward the trees.

"Go!" he whispered. She darted off.

He turned and crouched behind the massive smoker that had provided food for so many raucous gatherings, praying that Walker didn't choose this moment to become raucous himself.

Nobody was going to hurt his family...

TEXAS BODYGUARD: BRAX

USA TODAY Bestselling Author

JANIE CROUCH

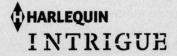

HARLEQUIN

INTRIGUE

Since this book is about family, it's dedicated to Kiddo #2.
Watching you on the court has always been one of
my favorite things in the world. Second only to seeing
the man you've become.

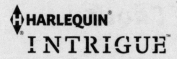

Recycling programs
for this product may
not exist in your area.

ISBN-13: 978-1-335-58255-3

Texas Bodyguard: Brax

Copyright © 2023 by Janie Crouch

For questions and comments about the quality of this book,
please contact us at CustomerService@Harlequin.com.

Harlequin Enterprises ULC
22 Adelaide St. West, 41st Floor
Toronto, Ontario M5H 4E3, Canada
www.Harlequin.com

Printed in U.S.A.

Janie Crouch has loved to read romance her whole life. This *USA TODAY* bestselling author cut her teeth on Harlequin Romance novels as a preteen, then moved on to a passion for romantic suspense as an adult. Janie lives with her husband and four children overseas. She enjoys traveling, long-distance running, movie watching, knitting and adventure/obstacle racing. You can find out more about her at janiecrouch.com.

Books by Janie Crouch

Harlequin Intrigue

San Antonio Security

The Risk Series: A Bree and Tanner Thriller

Omega Sector: Under Siege

Visit the Author Profile page at Harlequin.com.

CAST OF CHARACTERS

Brax Patterson—One of the four boys adopted as a teenager by Clinton and Sheila Patterson—the most charming and outgoing of them all. Owns San Antonio Security with his brothers.

Tessa Mahoney—Young woman who has lost everything and everyone important to her. Walker's mother.

Robert—Brax's biological half brother, Walker's father. Has a gambling addiction and always tends to be in trouble.

Walker—Tessa and Robert's infant son. Brax's nephew.

Weston Patterson—Most quiet and serious of the Patterson brothers. Often underestimated to others' demise.

Chance Patterson—Oldest of the Patterson brothers and the most strategic. The caretaker.

Luke Patterson—Gruffest of the Patterson brothers. Willing to do whatever needs to be done to protect his family.

Maci Ford—San Antonio Security's office manager.

Sheila and Clinton Patterson—Adoptive parents of the four Patterson brothers.

Prologue

Brax smiled at the couple sitting across from him in the San Antonio Child Protective Services office. They were talking with the social worker about him coming to stay with them.

They seemed nice enough. Older than dirt—at least forty or something. But the guy—Clinton— kept a protective arm around his wife, Sheila. He spoke respectfully to both her and the social worker, whose name Brax couldn't remember.

Of course, Brax knew Clinton could be completely fake. That under all that respect and protectiveness could be a guy who liked to hit, or worse, *touch*. But Brax was twelve now. He could outrun these old people no problem if he needed to. Get back out to the streets.

He'd lived on the streets last year, running from one of the care workers at a group home who had liked to touch. But being on the streets hadn't been as great as Brax thought it would be. Hiding from almost all adults, finding places to sleep where it was safe, having to figure out where he was going to get food…he hadn't liked any of it.

He'd survived, but there had been a little bit of relief when the cops had finally caught him and brought him back into this very office. It had been a different social worker then. Brax couldn't remember her name either.

They hadn't made him go back to the group home he'd run away from, so that was good. And now the people in front of him were talking about him living with them on a permanent basis.

Clinton answered something the social worker asked and Sheila looked over at Brax, returning his smile.

"Would you like to come and live with us?" she asked. Clinton and the social worker stopped talking and stared at Brax too.

Brax played it cool. "Do you have your own kids?"

Clinton shook his head. "No. We weren't able to have biological children. Plus, we've always wanted to adopt."

"Why do you want me? Why don't you want to get a baby like everyone else?" Brax kept the smile on his face as he asked it.

Any kid who lived in the system learned their defense mechanisms. For most it was a scowl or pretending to be tough and ready to fight. Brax had discovered that he could joke and charm his way out of a lot of bad situations. Or at least smile big enough that whoever was giving him a problem would let down their guard and he could run.

Big smile, fast legs. That's how Brax had survived since going into the system when he was nine, and it was how he would survive after Clinton and Sheila got tired of him.

"We're not really 'baby' people," Sheila responded. "We already have one adopted son. He's about your age."

Clinton nodded. "His name is Weston. We think you would like him."

Brax nodded, but didn't give the other kid much thought. He'd deal with that problem later if it was needed. Right now he wanted to get the question out that had been bugging him since he'd seen the couple walk in.

"Do you want me because I'm what your bio kid would look like if you could have one?"

Clinton was Black, Sheila was Latina. Their kids would be biracial like Brax, although Brax's mother had been Black and his father was white, not Latina. Maybe they wanted him as some sort of trophy or something. Brax wouldn't even mind that so much, but he wanted to know what situation he was getting himself into.

"My goodness, Brax, that's quite rude…" Ms. Social Worker sputtered.

Clinton held out a hand toward her. "No, it's okay." He turned to Brax. "It's very observant of you to even put that together so quickly. But no, we're not interested in you because you're biracial. Weston is Black. Luke, another boy your age who has stayed with us, is white. Race isn't what's important to us."

"What is important to you?"

Ms. Social Worker started sputtering again, but Clinton and Sheila ignored her.

"We are very blessed," Sheila said. "We have a big house where you can have your own room. We have money to be able to support a big family. And most importantly, we have love."

Clinton grabbed Sheila's hand, but kept his eyes on Brax. "And if you're interested, we'd like for you to give us a try. If it doesn't work, the group home or another foster family is always an option."

Brax stared at them for a long moment before giving them another smile and a nod. What did he have to lose? If he needed to take off, he knew how to do that. Knew how to survive. But for now he would give Clinton and Sheila and their little rainbow family a try.

It probably wouldn't last long. Good things usually didn't—Brax had found that out early.

Either way, he would survive.

Chapter One

At age eleven, Brax Patterson had endured seven weeks living on the streets by himself, hoping things would get better when he grew up. *If* he grew up.

Whatever he'd imagined during those long nights ignoring the hunger, trying to keep himself warm and alive, it hadn't been *this*.

A security company with his three brothers—none of whom had the same color skin as him, but who all had each other's backs and everyone knew they could count on the others no matter what.

They'd built a business where they could take the skills they'd learned from their pasts in the military, on the San Antonio Police Force, and even from being tossed around by the foster care system when they were younger, and use those skills to help protect others. San Antonio Security was on its way to becoming one of the most trusted firms in the San Antonio area. Although they did quite a bit of investigation, they specialized in protection—both bodyguarding and developing holistic systems to keep people safe.

Their office was rarely a quiet place, but that suited Brax just fine. Unlike his brothers, he thrived on the buzz of being around people.

On the whole, if all of them were in the office at once, that meant things were good. They were working, they were together, they were safe for the time being. Brax could smile to himself in relief when this was the situation.

Normally, anyway.

"If you would just leave my things alone, we wouldn't keep having this argument!"

Brax stepped into the hallway of their office, planning to get a drink from the fridge in the break room down the hall, but paused as he passed his brother Chance's office. Chance was running his hands over his head, lacing his fingers at the back of his neck. Brax had seen that move before. It was what his brother did whenever he needed to keep his hands still for fear of hurting something.

Or somebody.

In this case, it was somebody, though Brax knew Chance would never lay hands on a woman. None of them would—at least not in anger.

Maci Ford, their petite office manager, stood on the opposite side of Chance's desk, arms folded. "I told you. I wrote down everything you scrawled on that board before washing it off. I even took photos of it to keep the information for you."

"But why would you do that?" Chance's arms looked as if they'd jerk out of their sockets as he gestured emphatically toward the sparklingly clean whiteboard, which yesterday had been covered in a rainbow of words, arrows and circles—admittedly nearly impossible for anyone else to decipher.

"Because what happens if somebody walks in here and sees what you've written down? If they could read that chicken scratch of yours, that is. You never know what could happen. What if there was a break-in?"

Chance snorted. "Unlikely."

"Which isn't the same as impossible. Do you want somebody seeing the plans you're working on for this client's new security system? It's completely possible, and it's my job to make sure this office is run smoothly."

"By sending out invoices and tracking payment," Chance snapped. "Not by interfering with my work."

"Good morning." Brax smiled from the doorway, deciding to step in before the two killed each other. "If you keep going back and forth like this, you'll give me a sore neck. It's like watching a tennis match."

Maci jumped a little like he'd surprised her. She'd been too busy glaring at his brother to notice they had an audience.

"Sorry. I'll be going back to my desk." That didn't mean she couldn't throw one last exasperated look at Chance, who rolled his eyes at her and jammed his fists into his pockets.

Those two needed to get a room already.

Brax waited until they were more or less alone to jerk his head in her direction. "You'd better play nice. You know Luke says the office can't survive without her."

Chance rolled his eyes again. "Luke can't survive without her because of the filing he refuses to do on his own." Then, he smiled a little. "And we all know Luke loves everything right now."

"I guess that'll happen when a man gets engaged." It still felt strange, imagining any of them getting married. A bunch of confirmed bachelors—at least, that was what they'd been before the love of Luke's life had walked in one day a few months ago needing help to stay alive.

Claire had been more than worth the effort they'd put into protecting her, and not only because Luke loved her. She was a wonderful woman, brave and smart. And good for Luke.

Luke was in his office working on a case. Even when he was busy, there was a smile on his face. Brax wanted to joke about it but had decided to let the matter rest. It wasn't like Brax didn't have more than enough work to do himself. The exponential growth of San Antonio Security over the past year was a double-edged sword.

Weston passed his office around lunchtime and knocked on the open door. "How's that witness statement on the cartel case coming along?"

"Still need to finish writing it," Brax admitted, gesturing to what was in front of him. "I figured since the cartel trial isn't until later in the month, I should concentrate on wrapping up my current case and putting it to bed."

His latest case had involved a well-off woman who'd suspected her husband was guilty of cheating—among other things. She'd been right, of course, and right to believe she'd needed somebody watching her back at all times. Her husband had hired men to take her out so he could collect on her life insurance to cover his extensive, secret debts.

Brax had wrapped up the case, but not before his client had made a pass at him. More than one pass, in fact. He'd left her disappointed. The Patterson men were better than that. Professional.

And not stupid enough to get involved with married women trying to get back at their criminal husbands.

After tackling part of the mound of paperwork, Brax headed to the gym to work out the kinks he'd earned hunched over his desk all day. All four brothers kept themselves in top shape. It was one of the reasons a security business fit them all so well—it required engagement of both their minds and their bodies. They were all willing to endure both.

By the time he finished his workout, ate dinner and stopped back by the office to finish a little more of the never-ending paperwork, it was getting late. Time to head home. He enjoyed spending time with his brothers, but didn't mind being by himself. A little peace and quiet at the end of the day. Privacy. One thing he'd never had much of as a kid in one foster home after another.

Which was the reason he'd chosen to live in a house in the middle of nowhere with no neighbors close by. The most he heard at night was an owl's hoot or a cricket's song. He welcomed the nightly symphony as he dragged himself up the stairs toward his bedroom.

The ring of the doorbell brought him up short, tension coursing through him. He didn't get many visitors, especially at this time of night. His gun was already in the safe.

Another ring. He crept down the stairs, eyeing the door, grabbing a second weapon he kept hidden in a top kitchen cabinet.

Of course, if it was somebody coming to stir up trouble, they wouldn't ring the bell. They'd barge right in.

Still, it was worth caution.

Caution that didn't diminish when he heard the voice coming from the porch. "Brax? Let me in, man. I need you."

Brax muttered a curse. Of all the people to show up in the middle of the night, his half brother, Robert, would be the one. He put the SIG Sauer back in its hiding place.

He could ignore the bell, something he wouldn't consider for a split second if the man on the other side of that door was a Patterson. Luke, Chance and Weston were his real brothers. Much more than Robert, though he and Robert shared blood by means of having the same father.

Brax opened the door before Robert started shouting. "What are you doing here?"

"Hi to you too." Robert flashed his typical, greasy

smile. Under the porch light, Brax could see Robert's sweaty forehead, dark circles under his eyes, his skin paler than usual and oily black hair that looked as if he'd run his fingers through it over and over.

Robert glanced nervously over his shoulder, then back at Brax. "You going to let me in?"

"Do I have a choice?" Brax stepped aside, noting his brother's nonstop fidgeting. Hands he rubbed together, a twitchy jaw. Was he high on something? It wouldn't come as a surprise.

Robert hadn't exactly lived an honest life.

Brax and Robert looked almost nothing alike, something Robert had been quick to point out countless times in the five years since they'd known of each other's existence. Robert had also made it obvious he looked down on Brax's mixed race through little comments and slight aggressions against him and all of Brax's adopted brothers.

Funny how he showed up when he wanted something, though. Usually cash.

"What do you want?"

"There's been an emergency."

Again, no surprise. There was always trouble. It was difficult for Brax to muster interest. "What sort of emergency?"

Robert shrugged his thin shoulders and surveyed the room. Anything to avoid eye contact. "It's a long story. I've got a friend who owes me money. It's important that I get this money right away."

"I'm sure it is. But I don't see why you had to

come to me about it. Do you need protection? Help in some other way?"

"Yeah. Some other way." Robert held up a finger and went to the door, pausing with one hand on the knob. "Will you help me, bro?"

Bro? That made Brax's teeth clench.

The only reason he nodded his agreement was he knew Robert would never leave him alone otherwise. Besides, Brax was curious. He wanted to see how this would play out.

Whatever he had been expecting, it wasn't what Robert carried in one hand when he came back from his car. Not even close. "You're kidding me."

Robert looked down at the baby in the infant car seat. "Meet your nephew."

"My nephew? Since when do you have a kid?" Then, another thought, one that would've made him shout the house down if it hadn't been for the sleeping baby. "Are you alone otherwise?"

"Yeah."

"You left the baby alone in the car? What's wrong with you?"

Robert snorted. "He wasn't going to run away, you know." He dropped a diaper bag on the floor by his feet.

Brax blinked hard. Had he gone to bed, after all? Was this all a mixed-up dream? "You're going to need to explain a few things to me. When did you have a baby? Where is his mother? Why are you bringing him here to me? Where do I come in?"

"Wow. Where should I start?" Robert placed the

car seat on the coffee table. The baby stirred slightly but didn't make a sound. "His name is Walker. He's…uh…like four-and-a-half months old now or something."

Robert a father? It would've made Brax laugh in any other circumstance. "Okay. Why is he here?"

"I need you to watch him for a few days while I do what I have to do."

He was so cool about it. Like it was nothing. Like it wasn't the biggest favor one estranged half brother could ask another.

If this had come from any of his other brothers, it would've been one thing—a big thing, considering Brax had no experience with babies—but Robert?

"Are you out of your mind? I don't know the first thing about babies. You think you can show up here at this time of night after not speaking for, what, at least a year? And drop your son on my doorstep? What about his mother?"

"His mother's dead."

That took a little of the wind out of Brax's sails. "Oh. I'm sorry to hear that."

"Don't worry about it." Robert lifted a shoulder. "I never liked her that much."

Brax scrubbed a hand down his face. What could he possibly say to that?

Robert pointed to the diaper bag on the floor. "Everything you'll need for a few days is in there. Diapers, formula, all that stuff. He's a good baby. Everybody who's ever been around him says so. He doesn't cry all that much. When he's hungry, when he needs a change. Otherwise, he just sorta lays there."

Brax bit his tongue against what threatened to come out, knowing if he raised his voice it might wake the kid. *Maybe you leave him lying there because you're a terrible parent who probably doesn't care about him—or why else would you leave him with me?*

"I've got to go. I can't wait around while you keep telling me you can't do it. I'm in a hurry." Robert wiped fresh sweat off his brow. He wasn't pretending. The man was really and truly scared half out of his mind over something.

The reason he needed that money in such a hurry, no doubt.

The baby stirred again. This time, he let out a soft sigh in his sleep. It was the sigh that got Brax. Softened his heart.

"Okay." Brax held out his hands to try to get Robert to think this through. "Let's compromise. Why don't you stay here for a few days? I'll do everything I can to help you. I have resources through my company. You won't be in any danger here. Nobody would even think to look for you."

Robert, he noticed, didn't bother pretending there wouldn't be anyone looking for him. He ran his hands through his sweaty hair, jaw twitching, nostrils flaring. Not meeting Brax's eyes.

His answer came as a surprise. "Yeah, okay. We'll both stay here. Thank you."

Brax had expected another few minutes of argument, at least. He decided to take what he could get without questioning it. "I'll give you the spare room on the other side of the house. You look like you could use the sleep." Robert carried the baby and the bag upstairs and practically collapsed into bed, confirming Brax's suspicions. The man was exhausted. No telling how long he'd been on the run.

The baby seemed content in the carrier next to Robert on the bed, so Brax backed out, closing the door behind him. He headed back to his own bedroom.

He stared up at the ceiling for a long time. It took a while for him to finally stop thinking about the situation, wondering exactly what happened. About his brother, the baby, the dead mother. And what had brought Robert to his doorstep.

The sound of Walker's cries woke Brax in the morning. At first, he thought it was a dream. But then it all came back at once. He covered his head with a pillow in hopes of muffling the incessant noise.

"Robert!" he yelled. "The kid's crying his head off! Try taking care of him!"

He received no response. Not even the slamming of a door. The crying continued, getting louder.

A sick certainty took root in Brax's gut and started to grow. He got out of bed and walked down the hall, almost positive what he'd find before he even opened the bedroom door.

One baby, still in a car seat. The room stank of

whatever mixture was starting to soak through the kid's diaper and the little outfit he wore over top.

No Robert.

A note sat on the pillow. *I'll be back before you're out of diapers. I promise.*

Brax crumpled the note in his fist. He'd stopped believing in empty promises a long time ago.

Chapter Two

How did anybody survive a baby?

Three days. It had been three days since Brax had slept more than a few minutes at a time. Three days since he'd gone more than an hour without hearing a baby cry.

No. Not cry. *Wail*. The kid wailed until Brax's ears rang.

He kept expecting Robert to come back. That was the wildest part of all, waiting on somebody who'd been unreliable all his life to come back. To keep his word as the supply of diapers in the bag got lower and lower.

Diapers Brax had only figured out how to change by watching videos. Sad but true.

His brothers would've laughed themselves sick if they'd known. He could've told them, but it was smarter to stay quiet. Odds were whatever Robert was involved in wasn't exactly on the up and up. He was a father now, and there was no telling what would happen to Walker if Robert went to prison.

But three days was the breaking point. There was

nothing Brax could say to explain why he hadn't been to the office the past few days. None of his brothers would accept another excuse. They would come out to the house soon, and then he'd have a lot more explaining to do.

It was better to come clean and get the whole thing over with.

Which was what led him to strap the car seat into the back seat—again with the help of online videos—and drive to the office.

"What is *that*?" Chance's jaw nearly hit the floor when Brax entered, seat in hand, diaper bag slung over his shoulder.

Brax held a finger to his lips, but it was no use. The ride had calmed Walker, but the respite was too brief. Maci hurried over from behind her desk, hands over her mouth, when the baby started up again.

Weston darted out from his office at the sound of Walker's wails. "Where'd that come from?" He pointed to the baby, who Maci had taken from the carrier and held against her shoulder.

"Meet Robert's son, Walker." Brax sank into one of the chairs they kept out in the reception area and rested his head against the wall. "He likes to cry."

"Robert? Your bio brother, Robert?" Weston looked like he was having a hard time keeping up. "Where is he?"

"I'm not sure."

Chance followed Maci with his eyes as she walked up and down the length of the reception space with the baby, sort of bouncing him gently and patting his bottom with one hand. "So Robert showed up and left his baby with you?"

"Pretty much, though I barely remember. I don't think I've slept two hours over the past three days."

"I can take him to your office and try to get him calm," Maci offered. Brax thanked her and meant it with all his heart. At least the closed door muffled the sound.

Weston's confusion was clear in his dark eyes. "Did he tell you why he was doing it?"

"How long does he expect you to take care of the kid?" Chance asked, always logical and tactical. "Did he give you what you needed? Are you running low on supplies? Don't babies need a lot of supplies?"

Brax held up both hands in a silent plea. "One thing at a time. Robert said he needed to get money from a friend who owed it to him. That was all he'd tell me, and it's been three days without a word. He spent the night, but all that was left in the morning was Walker and a note saying Robert would be back before the diapers ran out. He gave me formula and clothes too."

"What about the mother?" Weston asked.

Brax ran a hand over his eyes. "Dead."

Weston and Chance both muttered a curse. None of them wanted to think of a baby growing up without a mother, although they all were testament that a woman giving birth to you didn't necessarily mean she would be your mother beyond the word *biological*.

"Okay. Let's run it down, see if we can find out

anything about Robert." Chance was already on the way to his computer by the time he'd finished speaking. Brax forced himself out of the chair and followed along with Weston. Walker was still crying, though somewhat softer than before.

"How did you figure out how to take care of him for the past couple days?" Weston asked while Chance ran Robert's name through their system.

"Internet. Thank goodness." Brax tried to muster a smile.

"You know you could've come to us for help."

"What do you two know about babies?"

Weston shrugged. "Nothing, but you didn't have to do this on your own."

"Here we go." Chance leaned in closer to his screen, eyes moving back and forth. "Big surprise. The last time he used his credit card was in Eagle Pass."

"Gambling," Weston muttered.

"Most of the activity on these cards the past few months has come from either there or Vegas," Chance confirmed. "He seems to be bouncing back and forth."

"Damn it." Brax rubbed his temples against an approaching headache. "I figured this was all about him owing somebody money, not the other way around. I doubt there's a friend involved. He has to run around trying to scratch together what he can now."

"Yeah, and getting out of town means avoiding whoever it is he owes." Weston shook his head. "Typical."

"Here's something interesting." Chance pointed to a couple of lines, which Brax read over his shoulder.

"We're not the only ones looking for him." Somebody else had put out feelers on Robert's card activity over the past few days. There was no way of knowing who without the digging getting much more complicated. The confirmation that someone else was after Robert was enough for the time being.

"What are you going to do about Walker?" Weston scratched his chin. "I think you should take him to Mom and Dad. You know how thrilled Mom would be to hold a baby, no matter whose it was."

It wasn't a bad idea. Not at all. Still… "I'd rather have him with me when Robert comes back. The fewer opportunities for Robert to slip away, the better."

Weston's scowl and Chance's sudden silence spoke to their disagreement. They were smart enough to stay quiet, at least. As tired as he was, he might've said something he'd end up regretting.

The crying grew louder when Maci left Brax's office. He turned in time to find her going through the diaper bag with one hand while holding Walker in the other arm. "What's up?" he asked.

"I was looking for a pacifier. His diaper's dry. When's the last time he was fed?"

"Right before I left the house with him. Burped him too," he added in case she was wondering. "I had to change my shirt thanks to his spit up."

"Daddy didn't pack any burping cloths?" Maci sighed, shaking her head. "Unprepared."

Brax wasn't about to ask what she was talking

about, not with the kid wailing like he was. They nearly shouted just to be heard over the noise.

Maci handed Walker over and practically stuck her head in the bag to look through. "What's this?" She nudged aside a few more diapers and undershirts, pulling a tag attached to the bag's lining.

There was a phone number written on it. "That's not Robert's number."

Maci looked at him. "Whose do you think it could be?"

"I don't know but I'm going to give it a try." He handed Walker back to Maci and pulled out his phone, dialing the number while she took Walker back to his office and closed the door.

"Hello?"

A woman's voice. She sounded troubled, concerned. Then again, he was calling from a random number. And how was he supposed to explain this?

"Uh, hi. This is going to sound strange. My name is Brax Patterson. Do you know a baby named Walker?"

She went quiet long enough to make Brax nervous. "Why are you calling me?" she finally asked.

He heard the suspicion in her voice and was about to try to ease it when Walker let loose with an ear-splitting scream. Even through the closed door, it rang out loud and clear.

"What's wrong with him?" She sounded as frantic as Brax felt.

"I don't know. That's why I'm calling. I found your number in his diaper bag and figured it was worth a shot. I'm his uncle. His father is my half brother. He left him with me for a few days, but I can't get him to stop crying."

"Have you tried swaddling him?"

"What's that?"

She let out a sigh. "I'll take that as a no. Swaddling is when you wrap the baby in a blanket. Do you have a blanket around?"

"Yeah, there's one in the bag."

"Okay. Here's how you do it. Think of it as a baby burrito." She walked him through the steps, making sure Brax knew to leave room for Walker's legs to move around. "He likes to be snug like that."

It worked. The second Walker was wrapped up tight, he calmed down.

"You're a miracle worker." Brax sighed into the phone, not caring that he probably sounded half out of his mind. "I can't thank you enough."

"He's always liked being swaddled. It calms him right away. It's a shame his father didn't know that."

Even if he had, Robert hadn't stuck around long enough to explain it. "How do you know what Walker likes? What's your name?"

She was quiet again, which raised his suspicions. Why was she so hesitant? "I took care of him for a little while. My name's Tessa."

She was a babysitter or nanny or something. That made sense.

"Thank you. You've pretty much saved my sanity. Not to mention Walker's lungs."

"I'm glad I could help."

As a last-second thought, he asked, "Have you heard from Robert?"

Another pause. "No, not any time recently. Is he in trouble or something?"

Brax decided to keep the specifics to himself. No telling who this Tessa was or who she knew. While his brother's protection didn't mean much to Brax, protecting Walker's father meant a great deal.

"No. Just waiting to hear from him. Would you do me a favor and take down my number in case he does contact you?"

Tessa read off the number as it appeared on her phone, and he confirmed it. "Can I have your address, just in case?" she asked. He didn't see any problem with that and, still feeling grateful for her help, recited the office address.

Finally, there was somebody from Walker's life on his side.

"Thank you, Tessa. You don't know how you've helped."

"I've heard him holler. I know how I've helped. Please, just take care of him." She sounded almost desperate.

"I will. I promise." She disconnected the call before he could say anything else.

"You can leave him in the car seat for now," he told Maci. "I'll keep him next to my desk. Maybe I'll be able to get some work done now that he's quiet."

Wishful thinking. While Walker didn't interrupt him, fatigue did. It took no more than fifteen minutes before Brax started nodding off. Maci was kind enough to bring him a cup of coffee, which helped some. But not for long.

He woke with a start at the sound of the doorbell out front. His gaze immediately darted over to the baby, but he'd finally fallen asleep and didn't seem ready to stir.

"Brax Patterson."

Brax shot out of his chair like he'd been fired from a gun. Had Robert finally come back? For the first time in his life, had he stood by his word?

No. It was a courier holding a thick manila envelope. "I'll need you to sign for these documents, Mr. Patterson."

Brax exchanged a confused look with Maci before accepting the courier's tablet and scribbling his name with the stylus. That earned him the envelope and its contents.

"Were you expecting something?" Maci asked.

"No." He opened it and withdrew a sheaf of legal documents. He spread the documents on Maci's desk, eager to find out what this was all about.

This had to be a mistake. He blinked hard, but that didn't change anything. "Robert has given me custody of the baby. I'm Walker's legal guardian."

Chapter Three

Tessa Mahoney could barely breathe as she ended her call with Brax Patterson. She folded the napkin on which she'd written his address with shaky hands and slipped it into her back pocket.

She couldn't afford to lose any of her jobs and had irritated her boss at the diner something awful when she'd taken the call, but it had been worth the risk. Even if she got fired.

"Good night!" she called out to the evening crew, waving as she stepped through the door and into the late-afternoon sunshine.

But it wasn't sunshine or fresh air that hit her awareness. It was the sense of being watched. A prickly feeling on the back of her neck.

Again.

This was the third or fourth day she'd felt it. The certainty that unseen eyes tracked her every move. Unnerving, especially since there was nothing she could do about it.

Including showing awareness. Her brown eyes darted back and forth as she hurried to the corner in hopes of catching the bus to her tiny apartment. At least she'd be indoors, away from the gaze of whoever currently watched her hustle down the street.

She couldn't let them know she knew. Nobody had to tell her that. It was instinct.

Ignoring her exhaustion, she sprinted toward the corner, waving her arms and begging the last person waiting to board to hold the bus for her.

The driver couldn't leave without her. She wouldn't be able to tolerate sitting on a bench out in the open feeling like someone was watching her as she waited for the next bus. She'd go out of her mind.

If she wasn't already insane.

"Thank you," she panted after leaping aboard, waving to the person who'd held the bus for her. She sank into a seat and closed her arms around herself in hopes of calming her trembling body.

This was all Robert's fault. All of it. She knew they were looking for him, which was why they were watching her.

Hilarious. As if he'd come to *her*. As if she'd let him.

And she was definitely the last person on the planet he'd share his plans with.

That didn't stop him from ruining her life from a distance, though. He didn't have many talents, but ruining lives was right up there at the top of the list.

She jumped with a strangled gasp as somebody behind her dropped their keys. Her nerves had reached their breaking point. She was losing it.

Breathe. There were times over the nightmare of

the past three months when she'd had to consciously remind herself of that. *Breathe. In. Out. Repeat.*

She would survive this. She'd survived the unimaginable already. If there was anything she'd learned, it was how strong she was. How much she could withstand without breaking. She'd get through this too.

Eventually, the people watching her would clue in to the fact she had no idea what Robert was doing or where he was.

At least the guy on the phone hadn't sounded bad—Robert's half brother, Brax Patterson. Different last name than Robert and Robert had never mentioned having a brother, but that wasn't a surprise. He had never exactly been forthcoming.

Brax had sounded like he was truly concerned about Walker—had swaddled him and gotten him to stop crying. That was good, right? But why wouldn't Brax know how to contact his brother if he was taking care of Walker? There were too many questions pounding inside her already aching head.

Arriving at her stop didn't provide much comfort. It meant exposing herself again since, if it was like the last few days, somebody was probably already watching. Waiting.

Or was she imagining things? Truly going out of her mind?

All questions vanished when Tessa reached her half-open front door. The door she knew she'd locked before leaving for her shift. A cold sweat covered her body, chilling her to the bone. Her stomach turned, threatening to give up everything she'd eaten for lunch.

Should she go inside? What if somebody was still in there? No, they probably would've closed the door to trick her into a false sense of security.

She nudged the door open with her foot, then stepped back. Her heart hammered in her chest as she expected somebody to jump out at her, to yank her inside the apartment.

The reality was just as bad. Someone had destroyed her apartment.

Broken dishes. Her plants thrown to the floor, dirt everywhere. The couch cushions and pillows strewn around, slashed open. Drawers emptied. Her clothes torn out of the closet and ripped to shreds. Her mattress on the floor.

Her apartment wasn't much—barely a living room and bedroom, a kitchenette and a closet-sized bathroom. But it was a place to rest her head, where she could feel safe. Or it had been. Every bit of safety she'd ever felt dissolved as she struggled with the sense of violation attacking from all sides.

Who would do this? And why?

"Oh no!" Terror flooded her system as she raced to the nightstand drawer where she kept her money.

Every dollar she'd sacrificed to save was gone. They had taken all of it. She sank to her knees, tears streaming down her cheeks.

The ringing of the phone jarred her. She didn't recognize the number but answered anyway. "Hello?"

"Do you like the redecorating job we did for you?" a cold, nasty voice asked.

Her eyes went wide, her heart hammering wildly against her ribs. Whoever had done this took pleasure in the pain and panic they had to know they'd caused.

"Why?" She hated the shaky whisper, hated knowing she was powerless against them, hated knowing there was nothing she could do.

"You know why. All you've got to do is tell us where Robert is."

She didn't whisper this time. She yelled. "I don't know!"

"Well, maybe it's a matter of jogging your memory. What about that? I wonder if somebody comes over to talk to you in person, you'll remember better."

She bit back a gasp before ending the call.

That wasn't an idle threat. She knew that much. People capable of breaking into her apartment, ransacking it and stealing her money were capable of anything.

Whatever Robert had done, she was paying for it. And she'd keep paying if she stayed here.

That realization forced her to her feet. Made her grab the bag thrown across the room at random, dig up the few pieces of clothing still whole and worth wearing and toss them inside.

Her knees threatened to give out, but she pushed herself forward, through the living room and out the door.

Someone rounded the corner of the stairs at the far end of the hall. A tall, hulking sort of man with a neck as thick as his head.

A wave of adrenaline crashed through her system. She darted back into the apartment and closed the door then wedged a chair under the door knob. Not that it would do much good. At best, it would buy her a few extra seconds, but she'd take them. She headed for the fire escape, praying that no one was waiting at the back of the building. The man in the hall hadn't seen her and wasn't hurrying so maybe she had a chance.

She moved as fast as her shaky legs would allow, nearly tumbling down the steep, rusted steps. When she reached the ladder, she looked up. Her window was still closed.

But it wouldn't be for long.

Sacrificing stealth for speed, she clambered down the ladder and into the alley behind the building. Which way should she go? It wouldn't take Thick Neck long to realize she had escaped and call his friends. She had to figure out a way to hide until they stopped looking.

Think, Tessa, think!

People. She needed a crowd to blend into. Would the pharmacy at the end of the block work? It had to, because there was no other option. She ran down the alley, not daring to waste precious seconds looking over her shoulder. If Thick Neck was following her, she would've heard him lumbering down the ladder, but all she heard was the traffic at the end of the alley.

She skidded to a stop and poked her head out just enough to check the sidewalk. All clear. She jogged out of the alley, rounded the corner and ducked inside the pharmacy, where it was hopefully safe.

With her head down, Tessa made her way to the back of the store, grabbed a magazine from the rack, and wedged herself into the corner across from the dome security mirror. Keeping her eyes glued to the mirror, she ran through her options.

Every nickel she had was in her pocket—the tips from her shift at the diner. The few clothes that had survived the "redecorating" were on her back or in the bag slung over her shoulder.

How far could she possibly hope to go?

She jumped when the phone in her pocket rang. It was the same number as before. Her palms were slick, making it hard to keep a hold on the device. There was no way she was going to answer. She powered it down. At least they wouldn't be able to track her using it if she left it off.

She needed a plan. There had to be something she could do. Somewhere she could go.

Like a gift from the guardian angel she probably didn't have, inspiration struck. The folded napkin still in her pocket, holding the address of an office building in San Antonio. That was only a couple hours from here.

A man who had called her needing advice about swaddling a baby… How bad could he be? And maybe he would find Robert and all of this hell could be over with.

Not all. Tessa rubbed her tired eyes. Even if Robert showed up again, her hell wouldn't be finished. She'd have to worry about that later.

She headed for the bus station with just enough cash to get her to San Antonio, hoping she wasn't making the worst mistake of her life.

Chapter Four

Thank heaven for swaddling.

Last night's fractured sleep was far from his usual state of unconsciousness, but it had been better than the few stolen minutes he'd been able to snatch the other nights since Walker had come into his life.

Brax was functional, but barely. And he wasn't ready for this. Any of it. He'd never planned to have a kid in the first place—even if he had, didn't a person usually have a little time to prepare themselves? To learn, to adjust their mentality?

A man didn't normally have a baby dropped into his life with no warning and no way out of the arrangement.

"What about calling a nanny service?" Maci bounced Walker slightly as she walked back and forth. Though Chance saw Maci as an annoyance and was grateful to have her preoccupied with a baby, Brax saw her as a saint.

"That's not a bad idea," Weston agreed.

Brax blew out a long sigh. "I don't know the first

thing about choosing a nanny. I don't know anything about any of this."

"That's the point of calling a service. They do the vetting for you. All you have to do is say yes or no once you meet the nanny they send." Maci shrugged. "It's an idea, anyway."

"It's a good idea." And when Weston decided something, that was that.

"Sure. Whatever." Brax leaned back into his chair, eyes closing. "If it means that I can get some sleep every once in a while and come to work without lugging the baby and all the stuff that comes with him, count me in. This can't go on forever."

Weston perched on the edge of Brax's desk, holding the paperwork. "I looked into this."

"And?"

"No big surprise, it's a mess." He pointed at the signature next to Brax's printed name. "Obviously a forgery."

"Yeah. Robert got a little creative there, didn't he?"

"And this Raymond Volver, the judge who signed it without even setting eyes on you? Very shady."

"That's Robert's cousin through his mom, and the only reason my half brother isn't in prison, I guarantee it. Ray cleans up after Robert all the time."

"I'm fairly confident an impartial judge will overturn this."

Brax nodded slowly, staring at the wall. "Yeah. But we all know what happens when guardianship is revoked. Walker goes into the system."

Weston put a brotherly hand on Brax's shoulder, a silent affirmation that no one wanted that to happen. "We'll track down Robert, figure it out. For your sake and for Walker's."

Brax put his hand on Weston's. Walker's soft noises floated in from the reception area where Maci paced with him.

And it was sweet. Fatigue and frustration weren't enough to keep him from smiling.

Walker was the only living blood relative Brax had besides Robert. Not that he felt alone. He hadn't for years, ever since his mom and dad had taken him in at twelve and shown him what family could mean.

Walker was his blood. Brax couldn't willingly, knowingly dump the kid into the foster care system. Not with his personal history.

By late morning, it was clear everybody had needed a break. Luke was still off in his personal happy place with his fiancée and would be in later. Chance was out shopping for baby supplies. Weston was following a lead for a client, though Brax knew leaving the office hadn't been necessary. Maci had volunteered to pick up lunch.

Brax was alone with Walker.

At least the baby was sleeping, swaddled up in his car seat. He was so much cuter that way. Was it wrong to think that?

A soft, female voice floated over from the reception area. "Hello?"

He was up in a flash, if only to keep whoever

was out there from waking Walker. "Yes? Can I help you?" he asked as he closed his door behind him.

She was beautiful. That struck him first. Petite with delicate features. Brown hair pulled back into a ponytail. A full mouth that tugged downward at the corners, and dark brown eyes that met his and held his gaze without flinching.

She looked confused. Tired. Troubled.

Instantly, something tightened in his chest. He wanted to help her. He *needed* to.

She opened her mouth, then closed it. Her brows lifted before drawing together. "Uh, yes. I think so?"

He waited, watching her. She carried a cheap fake-leather bag over one shoulder. A jittery hand plucked at the strap; her teeth dug into her bottom lip.

Nervous. His senses sharpened, tuned in to her every move, her every breath. The image of a wounded bird formed in his mind.

If he pushed too hard or came on too strong, the bird would fly away. "Would you like to sit down? Can I get you something to drink?"

"Um, I guess? Water?"

Was it a question? Why was she so uncertain?

He was about to ask that very question when a familiar noise started up from inside his office.

"Is that Walker?" she asked, eyes leaving Brax's face for the first time since they'd met.

Brax tensed. Just when he'd thought his protective instincts couldn't rev any higher. "Who are you? How do you know the baby's name?"

It was rare for anybody to relax in his presence

once he'd barked at them that way, but she did. "I'm Tessa. We spoke on the phone yesterday. 'Swaddling'?"

He relaxed. Maci must've called the agency she was talking about, and they'd probably reached out to Tessa since she'd taken care of Walker before. "Of course. Sorry for sounding suspicious. It's been a long few days."

"I understand." She pointed to his office, brows lifting in silent question, and he nodded.

She hurried toward the baby. "Hey, Walker!" Her sweet voice was soft as she unlatched the straps holding Walker in place. "How's my buddy? How come you're crying, huh?"

It was magic. The second the baby was in her arms, he quieted down. "There he is," she whispered, stroking his downy cheek with one finger and smiling down at him. "Missed you, buddy."

"You're incredible with him," Brax murmured. "He likes you."

She couldn't have been older than her early twenties, yet she handled the baby like she'd been caring for children for decades. Some people had the magic touch, he guessed, and thank heaven, again, Tessa had found her way to him.

By the time the guys showed up and Maci arrived with lunch, Tessa had fed and changed Walker and was rocking him to sleep in her arms.

"All right. Hold on." Luke stopped in front of Brax's office. "I heard there was a baby, but for some reason I still imagined it was a joke."

"Wow, that agency was quick," Weston muttered to Brax while Luke and Chance introduced themselves to Tessa.

"I know. Barely quick enough, though." Brax rolled his head back and forth, rubbing his neck. Why did his neck hurt? The damage a baby could do.

"Let's get you set up in the conference room," Weston offered. "If you don't mind working out of the office, that is."

"Not at all." Tessa looked at Brax with a smile. "This is unexpected. All this attention."

"Yeah. My brothers are always ready to jump in and help. It's just that we have to work, of course, and Robert dropped Walker on me without warning."

Tessa tilted her face away, but not in time to hide the way she grimaced at Robert's name.

Brax could understand that. It was obvious from the way she'd lit up when she'd seen the baby that she cared about Walker and couldn't believe Robert would do something as stupid as walking away from his child.

That was something they agreed on.

He left her in the conference room, softly singing to the baby in hopes of getting him to sleep. There was something so sweet and perfect about Tessa and Walker together that he couldn't stop looking over his shoulder at them. He forced his feet toward his office knowing the rest of him wanted to stay.

Chapter Five

Tessa finally had her son back in her arms.

It was all she could do to not break down sobbing, but with all the Patterson men watching, she knew that wasn't an option. They would ask too many questions.

Questions she didn't have answers for.

Tessa nuzzled Walker's downy, fuzzy cheek, breathing in his baby scent. Soaking it in. Drowning in it.

He'd grown so much bigger than she had imagined he'd be by now—and she had imagined it so many times. All day, every day. Every time she'd seen a baby in the street, in the diner or at the dry cleaner's, or in any of the houses she'd cleaned. No matter where she'd been working at the time, the sight or the sound or the evidence of a baby's existence had left her arms aching and her eyes stinging with tears.

He was so beautiful. He had her eyes, dark and deep. She had no doubt they held the secrets of the universe. All the wisdom in the world.

He'd shed the fine, wispy hair he'd been born with. What grew in now was her shade of brown, touched with a tiny bit of red that brought her mother to mind.

She kissed his forehead and closed her eyes and thanked God. She had her son in her arms again.

"I've missed you," she whispered, her mouth close to his ear. "I love you so much. Did you know that? I do. I do. Mama loves you."

This was an unimaginable gift. Worth the bus ride from Eagle Pass. Worth sleeping at the bus station. All so she could be with her baby for the first time in three months.

The longest three months of her life.

Two of the Pattersons were talking not far from the conference room. She looked up from Walker, frowning as she considered them. What was their story? What was this Brax person all about?

He'd called Robert his brother, but then he'd called the other Pattersons his brothers too. Did that mean Robert was related to all of them? Not only had Robert never talked about brothers, but the Pattersons were all of different races. Who was biologically related to whom?

Which one of them could potentially take her son away if they proved to a judge that Walker was related to them?

Who could she trust?

If Brax and Robert did share blood, there were more differences than similarities. Not only physically, though those differences had jumped out at Tessa the second she'd laid eyes on Walker's uncle. Brax had a commanding presence, tall and broad-shouldered, built like he took his body seriously and worked hard to stay muscular. He had a penetrating gaze that she guessed could inspire fear or confidence, depending on what he intended.

It seemed as if he didn't know she was Walker's mother. He thought somebody had sent her there—she'd overheard him saying something to one of the other men about an agency. That was fine for now, since she had no idea whether Robert had mentioned her.

Or what he might've said if he had.

No, there was no question about what he'd say. He would've told Brax what he'd told the judge. That she was a drug addict, an unfit mother.

And once again, he'd leave out the part where he'd drugged her and paid other people to call her unfit.

She held Walker a little tighter. There had been so many times when she'd feared she'd never have this opportunity again.

Why would that vindictive pig go to all that trouble to get custody if he was just going to run off and leave the baby with Brax?

Walker fussed like he felt the direction her thoughts had taken. How her blood started boiling the second she thought about that awful time. The powerlessness. The helplessness. It made her sick.

What had been Robert's plan when he'd destroyed her life and taken away the one good, pure thing that had ever been hers? His cruelty made no sense.

Walker whimpered. "It's okay, sweetheart," she whispered. Just looking down at him was enough to make her forget everything that had ever hurt her. Everything that had ever made her angry.

Now, she had to find a way to keep him. She wouldn't let go of him again. She couldn't.

Maci stopped in not long after Tessa had settled Walker down. The woman gave Tessa a good feeling, like she had an ally in this new world.

"How is he?" Maci whispered with a smile.

"Fine. Calm now." Tessa stopped short of thanking Maci for taking care of him. That would be a dead giveaway. Ally or not, Tessa had no way of knowing how much she could get away with.

"Good. He's a sweetheart. Just unhappy, I think. But he's happier now that you're here."

"I'm glad that's true." Tessa nodded past Maci. "What's the story here? Who are these men? It seems like they care a lot about a strange baby."

Maci smiled fondly as she took a seat across the table. "Brax's brother Robert gave him legal custody of Walker."

Tessa swallowed her fury. Why would Robert take Walker from her, then leave him with his brother?

"They're good men," Maci continued. "Private investigators. I think all of them were born with stronger protective instincts than most people. The work comes naturally to them."

That would partly explain why they took Walker's well-being to heart. But were they trustworthy?

"They're brothers?" she asked.

"Adopted, yes. All of them." Maci leaned in, whispering more softly now. "They were all foster kids, lost in the system until the Pattersons took them in."

That explained things, while somehow boosting Tessa's opinion of them. Was that why they wanted to take care of her baby? So he wouldn't get lost too?

Maci muttered a mild curse as she hustled to her desk to answer the phone, but Tessa was glad to be alone again so she could think.

They did security and private investigations. That meant the odds of her getting away with Walker were slim to none. They'd track her down without breaking a sweat, especially since she had no money and no friends in San Antonio.

Or anywhere.

"Hey."

Her head snapped toward the sound. Brax. Her cheeks flushed, though there was no way he knew what she'd been thinking. Guilt prickled under her skin, which made no sense. Walker was her son. Why should she feel guilty about wanting to keep him?

"Hi." She forced a smile. "I don't want to put him down. He might wake up."

He grinned. "Yeah, I understand. My arms are still sore from carrying him." He stretched them, bending at the elbows.

I seriously doubt arms that size could tire so easily.

What a weird thought to have.

"Where'd you go just then?"

The question stirred her from the strange, oddly aroused thoughts Brax's body stirred in her subconscious. "Hmm? Nowhere. I'm just…"

He came into the room and sat across from her. His body language was easy, friendly. One of the skills she'd learned waiting tables was how to read a customer's body language. Whether a guy was feeling particularly handsy that day, whether it would be better to put a little extra space between her body and his if she wanted to avoid having her rear end pinched.

Or worse.

Brax wasn't suspicious of her, which struck her as both touching and painfully naive. He didn't know who she was. He'd assumed. And every second she held her son, she was taking advantage of that assumption.

"Are you okay?" he asked, lowering his brows over his brilliant, penetrating eyes that seemed to look right through her. Was that a tingle running down her spine? Or a flash of guilt?

She shifted Walker to her shoulder. "Sure."

"It's just that when you first walked in earlier, I had the feeling you were in trouble somehow. Call it a professional habit, but I tend to pick up on those things. I honestly figured you for a client."

She nodded slowly, though her brain moved at top speed. Trying to figure out whether he was for real or if he was taunting her the way Robert had. Torturing her like a cat that had cornered a mouse.

Brax would never believe it if she told him what his brother had done to her. After all, she was a nobody. A stranger.

And if he knew she wasn't a nanny, he'd take

Walker away from her. She couldn't let that happen. She had to do whatever she could to keep Walker in her arms.

So she lied. "I was thinking about my parents, I guess. They've been on my mind lately. I was feeling sort of sad. Missing them."

"I guess being with Walker is only stirring that up more," he mused.

Was he playing around? She didn't think so—or maybe she didn't want to think so. It was all too confusing, and she was so tired.

"Yes. I guess so." She wanted to snuggle the baby closer but knew that might give her away.

"Well, I have nothing but good things to say about how he's responded to you so far. Between you and me, you're a godsend."

"Thanks."

This was it. The point where he'd drop the *but* on her. *You're great with him, but I don't need you. You're a godsend, but we'd better not see you sneaking around here anymore.*

"Are you free tomorrow?"

Her eyes popped open wide before good sense told her to cool her surprise. "Yes. I am."

"What about the rest of the week?" He offered a sheepish smile. Charming, even. "You see how busy we are around here. I've been scrambling for days trying to take care of him while getting my work done."

"Absolutely." She would've agreed to just about

anything as long as it meant being with her son. "Whatever you need."

It was almost a dream day. They'd even given her half of a sandwich and a cup of soup left over from lunch.

This was the safest and happiest she'd felt since Robert had taken their son from her.

But all good things came to an end. By six o'clock, the guys were preparing to leave for the night. She'd have to go too, even though she had nowhere to stay. She couldn't hide in the ladies' room until they locked up or camp under the conference room table.

"Good night. And thanks again for everything." Brax waved one last time before he walked off toward a car parked close to the building. Tessa walked slowly away from the front door, and with a glance over her shoulder to check if he was watching, slipped into the shadows of the alley between the buildings.

He didn't know she was watching. It was the best way to see how he treated Walker.

There was nothing to worry about. He was gentle with the baby, secured his seat in the car and spoke quietly to him. She couldn't make out exactly what he was saying, but the specifics didn't matter. He wasn't harsh or cold.

She breathed a sigh of relief before retreating deeper into the alley so he wouldn't see her when he drove past.

Where was she supposed to go now? She knew without counting there wasn't enough left from yesterday's tips to afford a hotel room, which was why she'd spent the night at the bus station.

She couldn't go back there. The cops might pick her up this time.

That left the alley. It was secluded enough. Clean enough. There weren't any rats, and it didn't reek of urine.

It would do for now.

She set her bag down along the wall and settled in with it against her back, guarding what little she had against potential thieves. Her brain hummed with the joy of having held her son again, the memories from the day replaying over and over.

She fell asleep with a smile, sitting upright in a narrow alley.

Chapter Six

It had been a dream week. A week spent soaking in everything about her son. Playing with him. Cuddling him. Singing songs to make him smile. Studying every inch of him as he slept.

Taking every second she could get.

She'd also spent the week sleeping in the alley and freshening up in gas station bathrooms. Washing her hair in the sink of one had been…an interesting challenge. But it had been worth it because she had her baby. She would live the rest of her life in an alley if it meant spending time with Walker. Watching him grow. Loving him.

Maci was always the first to arrive at the office, usually carrying donuts or bagels when she did. Tessa would follow her inside, answering questions about her night with made-up stories before quickly turning the tables and asking the office manager about her night.

Maci was thoughtful and friendly. And organized, considering how she kept four men in line. The Patterson brothers didn't seem like they'd be easy to wrangle.

Tessa had overheard Chance joking with Brax about how their mom would flip out if she knew there was a baby around and nobody had told her. Whoever she was, their mom had to be a special lady. Adopting four kids out of the foster care system wasn't for the faint of heart.

Tessa had moved into the break room. It was better than the conference room, more comfortable in there for both Tessa and Walker.

The fridge was right there, so was the microwave when it came time to warm bottles. She didn't love the idea of using a microwave and thought it would be healthier to warm his formula in a pan of simmering water, but people did what they had to do in tough times.

Like sponge bathing in gas station bathrooms.

At least her baby was eating and she was the one feeding him. That was what mattered most. She may have preferred taking care of Walker at a house, but she couldn't blame Brax for not trusting her alone with him.

The break room made it possible for her to get to know all the men as they wandered in and out. They each seemed caring and genuinely curious about Walker.

Weston had confirmed what Maci had already shared. "It means a lot to us that he has a stable upbringing," he'd confessed while nuking a cup of coffee. "We got lucky. Lots of kids don't. Not everybody gets adopted by loving people with the patience to undo years of damage."

Knowing they'd gone through so much hurt her heart.

But look how they'd turned out. They could've taken those years of damage and turned against the whole world. They could've taken their pain out on the people around them. Instead, they helped people. Protected them. It was their mission in life.

And it had made them hyperaware of what might happen to Walker if Brax didn't maintain guardianship.

Brax. Every time she thought about him, she fought back a tiny smile. What was it about him that made her react that way? Was it his voice? So distinctive she could home in on it even if she hadn't heard it for a few days. Or maybe his cologne? Her stomach tightened every time she caught a whiff.

All of her senses were focused on him at all times. Waiting for him to poke his head into the break room. Hoping to pass him in the hall.

He was easygoing, and he obviously took good care of Walker. That had to be why she was so tuned into him.

Easygoing or not, Brax would kick her out in a heartbeat if he ever learned who she really was.

It was clear he didn't like Robert very much. Whenever she mentioned Walker's daddy, Brax got a pinched look on his face like he'd just tasted something bitter. Did he know he reacted that way? Probably not. He'd never said much about his brother, but his body language spoke for him.

That didn't mean Brax would hear her out if she

tried to explain what Robert had done to her. Walker's best interests would always come first, which would mean kicking out the supposed junkie mom.

Tessa could respect Robert for putting her son's well-being above all else. Even if everything he said about her had been an outright lie.

Tessa scooched closer to Walker and bent to rub his back. He hated tummy time, but all of the articles she'd read said it was vital for his muscle development. Her body instinctively straightened as the intoxicating scent of Brax's cologne wafted her way.

"Come on, buddy," she urged Walker. "You can do it. Push yourself up on those arms of yours."

Brax leaned against the doorjamb and chuckled at the sight of his nephew fighting to push himself up off the floor. "That's right, little man. Work those biceps." Her heart skipped a beat when he flexed his own considerable biceps.

The best—or worst—part was he seemed oblivious. He wasn't trying to grab her attention. He wasn't deliberately showing off or flirting. He just happened to possess more charm than anybody should be allowed to.

And a body to match.

Robert had been charming at first, back when he'd been trying to get her into bed. He'd even made her believe he'd cared about her. Until proving how much he didn't.

That memory was like a bucket of ice water dumped over her head. She had to be smarter this time.

Brax's expression turned serious. Did he know what she was thinking? Of course not—he couldn't.

That didn't keep her stomach from turning into a sea of acid when he looked at her that way. Didn't stop her mind from spinning out in a thousand directions, trying to come up with a plan to get away with her son before Brax figured out who she was.

"I need to know how to pay you."

Oh, was that all? She almost laughed in relief but stopped herself in time. Laughter wouldn't be an appropriate reaction. "It's been such a joy spending time with this guy again, I almost forgot about that."

His frown deepened. "But you do have to get paid."

"Of course."

"I haven't received any paperwork from the agency, though. Nobody got in contact with me. I don't know how to set this up."

Right. The nonexistent agency.

"Well, I'm new in town." She shrugged. Did she look and sound confident in her lies? She had to. He was sharp. He'd see through lies. "Maybe my bank account hasn't finished getting set up yet. Why don't you pay me, then the agency will bill me for their cut?"

He would never go for it. Not when she'd only come up with that idea on the fly. No way.

"Sure. Would cash be okay this week, since your account isn't set up?"

Whoa. He was either deeply distracted or his powers of perception didn't extend very far. And she didn't care which.

"Sure, that would be great." It might mean buying a little food, some fresh clothes.

"Good. Tomorrow we'll settle up for the week?"

"That sounds good." Better than good. Could it be this easy?

He turned away, then pivoted to face her. "I don't even know where to contact you if I ever need you."

It was all she could do not to plant her face in her hands. She couldn't exactly give him the address of the alley. *I'm easy to find. Make a right out the front door, then another right when you get to the alley. Third trash can on the left.*

He had her phone number, though she'd taken pains to leave the phone off ever since that last day in Eagle Pass. But what about an address?

She scribbled down the first thing that came to mind, completely made up. Was there a Pine Street in San Antonio? Who knew? It was a risk she had to take.

"Great. Thanks." He slipped the paper into his pocket before running a distracted hand over his head. "Sorry. My mind's in so many directions right now. Word came in yesterday morning that a low-level drug dealer we helped put away jumped bail. We're trying to track him down before he gets too far away."

"Wow. That's intense."

He nodded, his jaw twitching. "Yeah. It's one of those things where we don't want the police involved since this isn't exactly a dangerous man. Drug dealer? Absolutely. But he's not a violent criminal. It'll be easier if we track him down first and bring him in. Once guns are involved…"

"I understand." Not only did it give her a clearer picture of the Patterson brothers, but knowing they were distracted by an important case gave her a little breathing room. No wonder he was willing to accept the first excuse about the agency that came to mind.

When closing time rolled around, Tessa prepared herself for another night in the alley. After Brax took Walker out in his car seat, she slid two bottles of water into her bag and followed him. Now that she knew there was pay coming her way, it was easier to let go of what little cash she had left. Maybe later tonight, she'd use the rest of her money to buy bread and peanut butter at the closest grocery store.

"Good night, buddy." She bit her tongue against the rest of what wanted to come out. *I love you. Mama loves you so much.* Words she whispered to him whenever they were alone.

But knowing she would lose sight of him for an entire fifteen hours made her want to say them anyway. Just in case.

"You need a ride?" Brax was all smiles, his usual charming self. So charming she wished she could say yes, that she wanted him to drive her home.

Only she couldn't because her address didn't exist.

"Oh, uh, no, thank you." As if someone had flipped a switch, her palms went sweaty. She licked her dry lips and hoped he couldn't read body language as well as she could. Because if he could, he'd know there was a problem.

"No, thank you," she repeated. "I like the fresh air. I think I'll walk."

"Oh, so you're not that far from here?"

"Nope." Did that sound as casual as she'd intended? Her blood froze in her veins when he frowned a little, like he was starting to put the pieces of something together in his head.

"Would you mind if I call you in early tomorrow morning?" he finally asked. "I don't know exactly how early. This case has us on our toes. There's no telling when or where we'll find this guy."

Her blood thawed. "Sure. I understand."

"So that's okay with you? I can pay double for the extra time."

Extra time with Walker and extra money? Like she would ever turn that down.

"No problem. I'll, um, keep my phone close by." But when he called, she'd have to be sure not to stay on the phone long enough for the men hunting Robert to use it to find her.

"Thanks." He granted her one wide, relieved smile before waving and turning toward his car. Her own smile stayed on her face long after he was gone, blood thawing even more.

THERE WAS NO such thing as getting decent sleep in an alley. Even if the alley didn't reek of urine and was fairly secluded. It was still dark without so much as a hint of light in the sky when Tessa's phone rang.

Adrenaline sent her bolt upright, her heart pounding hard enough to make her sick.

When she finally found her phone, it told her two things: it was two in the morning, and it was Brax who had awakened her from not-so-deep sleep.

"Hello?" She could barely push the word out of her mouth. If she didn't get a grip, he might figure out something was wrong.

"Tessa, I'm so sorry to wake you up like this, but things just broke with this case, and we think we know where to find our guy. It's something we all need to be there for. Can I come and pick you up at your place? I could drop you off at the office with Walker."

"No, no, it's okay. I'll meet you at the office in fifteen minutes." She put a hand over the phone when a car passed at the end of the alley.

"I'll be there in five."

She looked at the phone to confirm he'd already ended the call, ignoring all the messages from the diner wondering where she was.

She looked around in a panic before shoving her things into her bag: what was left of the bread and peanut butter and half a bottle of water. She couldn't let him see her makeshift home.

It happened so fast. She only realized she'd lost her grip on her phone when the thing hit the ground hard enough to break the screen.

"No!" Hot, frustrated tears welled in her eyes. She couldn't afford to be without a phone. How would Brax get ahold of her if he needed her?

She had barely reached the front door before he pulled up in front of the building.

He hurried around to open the back door and unstrap the car seat. "Thank you, thank you, thank you. You have no idea how much you're helping," he muttered. His arm brushed against her as he hustled to enter the code that unlocked the door.

"You have to do what you have to do."

If he thought it was strange that she'd made it to the office so quickly, he didn't mention it. "I'll be back as soon as I can. I promise. Thank you again for this."

"You're welcome." She took the car seat with a sleeping Walker inside.

Before he ran out the door, Brax pressed a kiss against her forehead. He didn't say anything, just left.

She reeled from the suddenness. And from how much she liked it. How could blood go from frozen to boiling so quickly?

She watched Brax peel away, staring into the darkness long after his taillights had faded. Mechanically, she turned out the lights, her head still spinning from Brax's kiss. It was innocent. Pure. So why had it hit her like a freight train? Why did it linger? She could've sworn she still felt his lips against her skin.

It had been so long since she'd had adult human contact. Even something that simple and quick. Robert hadn't exactly been big on affection or tenderness. Once he'd gotten her into bed there hadn't been a reason to pretend to be romantic.

He had even taken away her son. She'd been alone for months. Without a friend, without anybody.

Now she had her Walker, and in a simple, friendly way, she had Brax. Things were looking up.

The footsteps rang out a moment before a face appeared at the front window.

Tessa strangled a gasp and eased into the shadows, praying Walker wouldn't pick this moment to wake up. She studied the face she didn't know. Didn't want to know. It chilled her, those cold, hard eyes staring into the office.

Another man pushed him aside and tried to open the door. He pulled hard, but it didn't budge. Thank goodness Brax had taken the time to lock them inside. Thank goodness she'd turned out the lights. Thank goodness Walker slumbered peacefully.

She plastered herself against the wall, pushing deeper into the shadows, holding her breath like the men outside might be able to hear. Who were they? Not friends of the Pattersons—she would've bet good money on that if she'd had more than eighteen cents left to her name.

"I followed the signal," the one at the door growled. "You positive it died?"

"Yeah." The man at the window nodded, throwing a filthy look inside the building like his frustration was the building's fault. "Maybe there was something wrong with the equipment. Why would she be here in the middle of the night?"

Tessa's stomach flipped. They were there for her, probably having traced her phone in the short time she'd used it. Wanting to be available for her son, available for Brax, had led them to her. It hadn't felt like it at the time, but her smashed phone had been a blessing in disguise. What if she had left the phone on?

She gasped softly as Walker stirred in his car seat. With one eye on the men outside, she lowered the seat to the floor, unlatched the straps, and clutched him to her chest. "Shh, baby," she whispered, holding him close, hoping her heartbeat and contact with him would keep him quiet.

Holding her breath, holding her baby, she watched the men. She was afraid to move or even breathe. One of them tried the door again and examined the lock before pulling hard.

Finally, they muttered a few vile words and stalked toward a nondescript car. Just as she had with Brax, she watched the taillights disappear into the night and she was able to breathe easily again. "Thank you," she whispered into the otherwise silent room.

Her knees wobbled as she made her way to the break room. There were no windows there. They would be safe. Nobody would be able to find her here. Nobody would be able to take her son away.

Chapter Seven

What had he been thinking, kissing Tessa like that?

That was hardly what Brax needed to be worried about on the way to the trailer where Nick Lomax's girlfriend lived with their three-year-old son.

No, Brax should have been thinking about the case. About surrounding the trailer and getting Nick to go with them before anything hit the fan.

Especially with a woman involved. Not to mention a little kid.

Yet kissing Tessa was all he could think about as he'd sped out of town toward the rendezvous point. He tried to tell himself he'd been distracted, in a hurry to meet up with the guys. That it was important that Nick didn't feel threatened, and Brax was always best in situations like this.

But the lips that were supposed to coax Nick out of the trailer still burned from the sweet, innocent kiss he'd pressed to Tessa's forehead like any dutiful husband leaving his wife and child at home before heading to work. That should bother him. So why didn't it?

He ran a frustrated hand through his hair. How

was he supposed to concentrate on helping Nick out of this situation without his family getting hurt if he couldn't stop thinking about Tessa?

What if she quit because of this? He'd stepped over the line. Not too far, but far enough. Assuming a sort of intimacy they didn't share.

He wouldn't have blamed her if she wanted out of their arrangement. Like it wasn't bad enough he'd called her at two in the morning and pulled her out of bed. Like he wasn't already making her life difficult.

He made it to the meeting spot roughly a half mile from the trailer park.

"About time you showed up." Weston gave him no time to defend himself before gesturing to the tablet Chance held. "We were discussing how we plan to surround the place."

"I'll take point," Brax decided. "If I'm going to be the one to talk him out of there, that's where I need to be."

"I'll flank on the right, Luke on the left," Weston announced. "Chance, you take the rear in case he decides to escape through a window. Keep eyes on the structure—some of them have doors in the floor. He could slip out and try to make a run for it while we're all focused on the front."

"Everything okay?" Luke caught Brax's eye before hitting him in the face with the beam of his flashlight.

"I was okay before you blinded me." Brax held up a hand in front of his face. "I'm fine. I had to take care of things with Walker first."

"Right. Of course." Weston sounded apologetic, at least, though he didn't offer any true apology for his remark. Not that Brax expected one.

It was nearly a quarter to three by the time they rolled to a stop and exited their vehicles alongside the fence that defined the trailer park's boundaries. Keeping his flashlight low, Brax kept an eye on the windows as they approached their target.

"We don't know whether the girlfriend and kid are inside," Chance reminded them through the comm system as he took his place behind the trailer.

Brax would've bet on it. There were toys in front of the trailer. An inflatable kiddie pool. And a car parked close by. The entire family was probably in there.

He kept this in mind as he crept to the door, waiting for visual confirmation that his brothers were in place before banging his fist against the metal. "Nick Lomax. Come on out."

It was important to keep his voice strong, firm, but low enough not to shock or startle Nick—or the neighbors, who if they chose to get involved could complicate things.

A light went on in the rear. The sounds of tight, frantic whispering filtered out through the screened window.

"Nick, we're not here to hurt you or your family. But you can't keep running. You know you'll get caught, and it'll be that much worse for you when you do. Don't put your family in harm's way like this."

There was movement inside. A lot of it. Things

getting pushed around, doors opening and closing. The man wasn't exactly skilled at making a silent getaway.

"Nick." He rapped harder on the trailer. "This doesn't have to end badly. Come in with us, and we'll get it worked out in your favor without having to involve the cops."

Weston gestured to the window where Nick was visible. His voice rang out in the night air. "I ain't going back. I'll shoot you dead before I let anybody take me back."

Brax's throat tightened, and he fought to control the tension ratcheting up inside him. One of them had to remain calm and in control.

"It doesn't have to be that way," he assured the man. "Notice how we didn't bring bounty hunters or cops with us. We don't want to put Darlene or your son in danger."

"They didn't do nothing wrong!"

"We know that. Which is why we're only here to bring you back in. You missed your appearance and a warrant will be issued for your arrest. You know that. We have the trailer surrounded. It's for the best that you come out now without putting up a fight."

The baby cried. Not a baby, not anymore, but young enough to instantly bring Walker to mind. What would he do if he were trapped in a trailer with Walker, knowing there were armed men outside? Whatever it took to ensure the kid's safety, without a doubt.

But how could he say goodbye to him? What if

the entire reason he'd run was to be with his child, who he'd now be torn away from?

"Nick, I know you want to be with your family. I get that. But you have to keep them in mind. You're right. They didn't do anything wrong. They're innocent in all this. But you're dragging them into it now. Don't you see that?"

Darlene's crying mixed with the kid's twisted the knife in Brax's chest. "You've got to do what's best for them right now, Nick. Which means coming with us. Not putting up a fight. We don't want any gunfire with a woman and child in the house. And we don't want to see you get hurt. If you serve your time, you'll be with your boy in a few years. You try to run and you risk much worse."

"Bathroom window opened," Chance whispered in his earpiece. "Looks like he's going to make a run."

Weston went around back to prepare for it.

Brax muttered a curse. This was not the way things were supposed to go. "Nick, I need you to talk to me. Where are you? Come on, man. For your son."

"Please. Don't shoot him." That was Darlene near the front door. Her voice was thick with emotion.

"We have no intention of opening fire. I promise you that. But I need him to come out without a weapon. We will defend ourselves if it comes to it."

"She'll convince him," Luke predicted.

Brax wasn't so sure. The man didn't want to go to prison. Anybody could understand that.

"For your boy," he nearly begged. "Let him grow

up knowing he has a daddy who loved him enough
that he didn't do anything stupid at a crucial moment.
Let him look forward to seeing you again, Nick. You
can put this behind you someday. But you have to
be smart now."

His weapon was at the ready, in case their man
came out shooting.

The lock flipped. "I'm coming out. I'm unarmed.
Don't hurt my family."

Brax could've collapsed with relief. "We won't
hurt any of you." Then, more quietly for the sake of
his brothers, "He's coming out through the front."

Chance and Weston joined him and Luke in time
for the door to swing open. "Hey, Nick," Brax offered. "It's good to see you."

By the time he had Nick back in custody and
awaiting his rescheduled court appearance, it was
nearly dawn. Would Tessa be worried? He hoped
she'd managed to get some sleep—the sofa in the
reception area was comfortable enough.

Yet she wasn't out there when he arrived at the
office. He entered the code to unlock the door and
turn off the alarm, his gaze sweeping the floor as he
did. Where was she?

For the briefest moment, just a flash in the back
of his mind, Brax imagined Tessa taking Walker
and running. Disappearing into the night while he'd
been miles away talking a bail jumper out of doing
anything stupid.

But no. If she'd left, he would've gotten an alert
that the alarm had been tripped. Knowing she had

to be around somewhere, he could breathe easier as he walked from one room to another looking for her.

He found them in the break room on a pile of blankets on the floor. Tessa slept curled around Walker like she was protecting him.

Brax crouched beside them, content to observe for a moment or two. Walker slept peacefully, his mouth curved into a little bow. What did babies dream about? Diaper rash? No, not if they looked as sweet and comfortable as his nephew did.

Tessa didn't look so peaceful. Her delicate brows were drawn together, her forehead pinched like she was in pain. What was she dreaming about? Nothing good, that much was clear, especially when she whimpered like a wounded puppy.

It would've been mean to leave her that way any longer. Being awake had to be better than whatever was happening in her dream.

"Tessa?" He hesitated to touch her after the stupid kiss earlier, but she wasn't budging. With a hand on her shoulder, he whispered her name again.

Her eyes flew open, and her body jumped. "What? Huh?"

"Shh, it's just me. It's Brax. Everything's okay." He stopped short of taking her into his arms to calm her down—barely, since that was all he wanted to do. To hold her and calm her and let her know everything was okay.

She blinked hard, holding a hand to her forehead. "Brax? Oh, I'm sorry."

"No, I'm sorry. I startled you."

"It's just that I got a little freaked out, I guess." She offered a weak little laugh. "All alone here, middle of the night, that sort of thing."

"I'm sorry. I didn't think about that when I asked you to spend the night here. It must've been creepy." He was careful to speak quietly, and not only for the baby's sake. Tessa was still spooked.

"At first," she admitted with a shaky sigh. "But things turned around. And he was an angel the whole time."

"I'm glad to hear that—though I'm sorry you slept here on the floor. It couldn't have been comfortable."

She shrugged. "It was fine. And it's only been a few hours. Not all that long."

Before he could dispute this or apologize yet again, she asked, "Did everything turn out okay?"

It took a second for him to understand what she was talking about. "Oh, yeah. It went as well as it could. We took the guy in before anything went wrong."

"That's a relief." She ran a hand over her face, yawning. "What a night for both of us, I guess."

What would he have done without her? "I can't thank you enough. I wish I could tell you this sort of thing will never happen again, but I don't like making promises I can't keep."

"I understand. You have an unpredictable job. And I like spending time with this one." She rubbed Walker's back with a gentle hand, smiling softly.

The question was out of his mouth before he could even consider thinking twice. "Would you like to make this a full-time arrangement?"

She gulped. "Full-time?"

Now that he'd gotten started, he couldn't stop. It was like somebody had pulled the plug from a drain.

"You could move into my house—it has three bedrooms, with two on the other side of the house from mine. No strings attached. You're free to say no. And I hope you know I would never dream of doing anything to make you—"

"Yes." She touched his knee with a shy smile, cutting off the flow of words pouring from him. "Yes, I would love to do that. Thank you."

That one touch lit up his insides and convinced him he'd made the right choice.

As long as he could learn to live with a woman and a baby in the house without driving them both insane.

Chapter Eight

"Happy birthday, dear Walker…" Tessa leaned over to kiss her son's forehead. "Happy birthday to you."

She snuggled him a little closer, laughing at herself for even thinking of singing Happy Birthday to a five-month-old.

"It's your five-month birthday," she whispered with another kiss before putting him in his highchair. It was brand new, one of many things Brax had purchased over the past two weeks. "You're getting to be such a big boy now."

Walker waved his fists, smiling from ear to ear. Even if he couldn't understand what she was saying, she could tell he liked the sound of her voice.

So she talked to him all day long. Anything to make him happy. It didn't hurt that it made her happy too. When she wasn't talking to the baby, she was singing. Every song she knew, one after the other.

Not only because he enjoyed it, but because she did too. It had been so long since she'd sang or had any reason to sing. Being with Walker gave her that reason.

More than that. It was feeling safe in a beautiful home set on lots of land without a neighbor in sight. Plenty of trees, tons of sunshine. Room inside to move around. No sense of claustrophobia, no sounds and smells from neighbors on five sides of her apartment.

This was exactly the sort of home she'd always wanted. It was like living in a happy dream. Waking up, caring for her son, loving him openly.

And Brax. He was great too.

Not that she loved him. Not even close. But being around him was wonderful. There was somebody to look forward to seeing at the end of the day. To say good-night to before heading to bed. Somebody to share Walker's latest superhuman achievement with.

Because they'd agreed early on that Walker was the smartest and most talented child who had ever existed in the history of the world.

The thought made her smile as she fixed herself breakfast. Brax had left earlier than usual—she liked to at least have coffee with him in the morning to go over Walker's schedule. When she should expect him home, whether he should pick up anything at the store along the way.

The simplest, most mundane conversations. Yet they meant the world to her.

"I was lonely for a long time, buddy." She glanced over at Walker, who was in the process of trying to eat his fist. "I didn't know how lonely until now, since I'm not lonely anymore. Now I can see."

She could also see why it had been so easy for

Robert to get her into bed. He'd probably spotted a big old target in the middle of her forehead when they'd met. No challenge whatsoever.

It had been that way since the accident. Losing one parent would have been rough enough, she guessed, but both at once? At the age of twenty? She'd been thrust into a new life overnight.

No more comfortable house. No more family dinners. No more security. No more love.

Walker banged his fists on his tray, happy with himself. The noise shook her from dark thoughts. "You're into making noise lately, aren't you?"

He banged on the tray again like he was answering her. "You know, your timing is uncanny sometimes."

The phone rang after lunch. Brax's landline, so old-fashioned in a way, but helpful since she'd broken her phone. He checked in at least once a day to see if everything was okay.

She realized on answering that she had even come to look forward to these little calls.

"Hi." There was no wiping away her goofy smile. Good thing he couldn't see her.

"Hey." His deep, rich voice held a touch of laughter in it. He was almost always in a good mood. Charming, funny. Pretty much the polar opposite of Robert. "How's it going there?"

"The usual. Plenty of peace and quiet now that Super Walker is down for a nap. He'll be an excellent drummer someday, I think. Great rhythm when he's banging things together."

"Remind me to never pick up a drum set."

She giggled. "Pots and pans. Wooden spoons. You do the math."

"I was never much good at math." They shared a laugh. "Hey, I meant to tell you. I took your phone over to a guy who runs a shop a few blocks from here. He said it should be fine in a couple of days."

"He'll fix it for me?"

"Well, for me," he chuckled. "We've done a little security work for him in the past. He said he sees phones like that all the time and can almost always fix them up."

"Wow. It was so sweet of you to go to the trouble."

"No trouble at all. Just think, you'll be able to take some time away from the house now since you'll have a phone you can use to get in touch if you need anything."

Right. Because that was her excuse to stick close to Walker. Not having a car was one thing—Brax had already offered to lend her his car if she wanted it.

Not having a phone was another. There weren't pay phones on every block like there'd been in the old days.

Brax, being the protective man he was, hated the idea of her going out without a way to call if the car broke down or some catastrophe occurred.

Being the absolute sweetheart he was, he thought about her comfort and happiness all the time. As if they truly mattered. And he was dead set on her taking time for herself, not knowing she had nowhere to go and no one to see.

"Thanks," she said, though her heart wasn't quite in it. The fact that she was afraid to be out of Walker's presence for even a little while didn't lessen the kind gesture, so she injected a little sunshine into her voice. "I'll owe you a special dinner tonight to make up for it."

He groaned. "You're speaking my language, though I don't see how you have the energy after taking care of the baby and the house."

She was used to being on her feet all day, waiting tables and cleaning houses and doing anything else she could to make ends meet. Walker was still at the stage where he slept a lot, giving her time to check off her daily tasks without a problem.

"So, what's for dinner?" he asked.

"It's a surprise," she teased. "So don't be late."

"I love surprises. See you at six fifteen on the dot," he promised before hanging up.

She clutched the handset to her chest with a grin as she remembered how surprised Brax had been that first night she'd scrounged around the kitchen looking for dinner ingredients, hoping for inspiration. He'd gotten used to a lot of frozen meals and takeout, evidenced by the number of packages in the freezer and containers in the fridge. The aroma of a home-cooked dinner had practically sent him drooling.

It was a pleasure for her to watch him as he enjoyed her cooking. She knew she was a good cook thanks to the time in the kitchen bonding with her mother once she was tall enough to reach the stove.

It felt good knowing she could provide a little something for him after he'd given her so much.

He would never know how much he'd given her. He *couldn't* know.

The knowledge that this wasn't real always sat at the back of her mind. He could find out about her at any time. It was why her heart leapt every time the phone mounted on the kitchen wall rang.

He could be calling to say hello, or he could be calling to say goodbye, to tell her to get her things together and get out.

As it was, he'd been suspicious when she'd suggested he pay her in cash every week. "I don't like paying the check and direct deposit fees at the bank." She'd shrugged. "Every penny counts."

He'd let it go without questions, though it had been clear from his frown that he thought it was strange. How many more strange things could she say or do without him demanding answers? Soon he would want to know why he hadn't heard anything from the agency about paperwork.

Which was why she'd keep her head down and save every cent she could. Eventually, she'd have enough money to hire somebody who could clear her name—ironically, San Antonio Security was exactly the sort of business to do something like that.

It was impossible. She couldn't even hint at needing their help. They would take Walker away. She couldn't lose him again.

But she couldn't fool Brax forever. The sooner she had enough money saved, the better. What if Robert decided to come back all of a sudden? That would be the end of everything.

And it could happen at any time. The sense of an anvil hanging over her head followed her wherever she went. It could drop whenever, wherever.

Walker's soft cries from his crib filtered through the monitor. It was like he felt her thoughts sometimes. He had a way of breaking in before she went really dark and depressed herself.

After changing him, she picked up a blanket and walked him downstairs. "Let's go outside and get some fresh air and sunshine." That was what she needed, a way of recharging her spirits.

It was their late afternoon ritual. He'd wake up from his nap, and they'd lie out on the blanket for a while basking in the sunshine. It was the only sort of life she wanted to live. Lazy afternoons with her son enjoying the last of the sun's rays before getting dinner started.

And saying hello to the man of the house when he got home.

Tessa flinched when the hair along the back of her neck stood straight up. She raised a hand to the area, rubbing like that would help ward off the sudden chill.

Walker continued gazing up at the clouds and babbling while she sat up, her head on a swivel. There was nobody out there. No neighbors near enough to make out their houses in the distance. No passing or parked cars.

Why did it feel like there was somebody watching her?

She hadn't felt this way since Eagle Pass. Her instincts had been dead-on then, and those same instincts were screaming at her now. But Eagle Pass was more than two weeks behind her. There hadn't been any trouble since the night she'd spent at the office when those two men had come looking for her.

"I'm letting my imagination run away with me," she murmured to Walker, still scanning the horizon in all directions. "Come on. Let's go back into the house."

Even if it was nothing more than her overactive imagination—and it had to be—she rushed Walker inside and locked the door behind them.

Chapter Nine

"Nothing all day. Movement and shadows mostly but nothing verifiable. Nobody in or out."

Brax groaned, rolling his head around on his stiff neck. "I never knew sitting still and watching an apartment could leave me aching the way it does."

"You don't get up and move around enough. I warned you about that." Weston would know, having performed his fair share of stakeouts when he'd been with the police department.

"I can't shake the feeling that the second I look away for anything more than an emergency, I'll miss something important."

"I get it." Weston took a seat where Brax had spent the day in the apartment they'd rented across from that of a suspect they suspected in a string of home invasions. When the San Antonio PD had thrown up their hands in despair after a dozen invasions left them with no evidence and no real suspects, one of the victims had hired the Patterson brothers to look into it.

Within two weeks, they'd found their prime suspect and had been staking out his apartment ever since, keeping track of his movements and of any visitors.

"I guess you'll be on your way home now." There was a hint of a smile tugging Weston's lips as he looked Brax up and down. "A hot, hearty meal waiting for you. A woman to serve it. You've got it made, brother."

Brax waved off Weston's obvious joking. "Please. She has time on her hands, and she likes to cook. I'm not getting any ideas about it."

"Why not?"

"Because she works for me. Enough of the devil's advocate." He cleared his throat before changing the topic. "Anything new about Robert?"

"Nothing we didn't find before. Though truth be told, we've been busy."

"Yeah, and I've been doing all right with Tessa— and Walker," Brax added, but it was too late. The spark in Weston's eyes said everything.

"Doing all right with the nanny. I wonder what Mom would think about that."

"Okay, enough." Brax held up his hands in mock surrender. "Fact is Tessa is twenty-two years old. A nine-year age difference is sort of substantial."

"I'll grant you that. But don't pretend you don't look forward to getting home and seeing her. You smile almost as much as Luke does nowadays. Honestly, I don't recognize either of you."

"Funny guy. You know, Walker might have something to do with that."

He did. Now that those early days were over and there was no more panic, Brax had been able to relax and get to know his nephew. The kid was adorable when he wasn't screaming. Tessa was good with him.

It cracked him up to no end to see the baby watching as the two of them held a conversation. He was so serious, studying their mouths with his little face scrunched up in concentration. He'd be a smart kid, no doubt.

Unlike his father.

"So? Have you spied on her while she's alone with the kid?"

Brax bristled at this, though there was a slight amount of embarrassment behind it. "How'd you guess?"

"I'd wonder about you if you didn't. Where did you hide the cameras?"

"One in the kitchen, one in Walker's room."

"And?"

"And she was great with him the entire time. I only did it for the first couple of days. Just to satisfy myself that she was as good to him in private as she was in front of me."

"Of course."

He didn't tell Weston about her singing. About the endless games of peekaboo. How she talked and talked to the baby—the audio went in and out depending on her volume and the room she was in at the time, but her facial expressions said it all.

She loved Walker, and it showed.

If anything, that only helped him like her more.

They had something they loved in common. Something they worked together to nurture. Something that made them laugh at the dinner table with his comical facial expressions and sudden outbursts.

Those evenings with Tessa had become the highlight of his day.

Which meant he had to get moving if he was going to enjoy another one. "I'd better go. She might worry if I'm late."

"She's got you following orders already."

"Watch it," Brax warned, and he was only half kidding. There were limits to joking around.

"Can I offer you a little brotherly advice before you go? In all seriousness." When Brax nodded, Weston continued. "You have a lot to think over. Plans to make. Decisions to come to."

"I know I do. And once my testimony against the cartel is delivered, I'll have the emotional bandwidth to consider the rest of my life. I'll start making those plans once that's all wrapped up."

"Do you think Tessa might fit into those plans?"

He only shrugged a shoulder and grinned before saying goodbye. There was only one word to answer that.

Yes.

With each passing day, she had worked her way deeper into his heart.

He already regretted his original attitude toward Walker, who now gave him reasons to smile, to relax and enjoy life. His heart had already changed.

What about having a woman to come home to?

His woman. Not a nanny or babysitter. Somebody whose face lit up when he walked through the door.

The way Tessa's did.

"No way," he warned himself. Hadn't he promised there wouldn't be any funny business? The last thing that poor, haunted woman needed was to feel pressured. Like she had to sleep with him if she wanted to keep her job.

There were times when he wanted nothing more than to wrap her in his arms and beg her to tell him what was wrong. What she hid about herself. Why she sometimes averted her eyes when they touched on the topic of Robert or her life before meeting Brax.

Whenever that happened, he recalled the wounded bird who'd first walked into the office and given him the sense of somebody needing help. Protection. Safety.

His cell rang, the sound echoing through the car's sound system. He imagined it was Tessa calling from the house asking him to pick up something on the way.

It wasn't. The call came from a very different number. "District Attorney Morgan. I just mentioned the cartel case to my brother a few minutes ago. Your ears must be burning."

He could normally charm just about any woman with little to no effort. It was a talent he chose to use for good instead of evil.

Janice Morgan didn't so much as snicker, which was how he knew they had a problem even before her voice rang out. "Remember that shopkeeper? The main witness we have lined up for the trial?"

"Of course. Older guy, right?"

"Mr. Henderson is in his fifties, yes. And he just had a heart attack. I got word from the ICU just a few minutes ago."

Brax muttered a curse under his breath. Of all the things...

"Did they give you an indication of an expected outcome?"

"No." She sighed. "But I don't think it matters much either way as far as the case is concerned. He's set to testify in ten days, and he's in the ICU this very minute. No way is he going to be strong enough for court. You don't face down Prince Riviera and his entire gang when you're at half strength."

Prince Riviera. The name still made Brax roll his eyes, even knowing the sort of filth and degradation the man and his gang were capable of. The Riviera cartel practically owned the border between west Texas and Mexico and had since before any of the Patterson brothers had been born.

"Honest question—do you think the cartel is capable of this?"

"Giving the man a heart attack to keep him from testifying?" She sighed heavily, the sound of a woman completely run down by work. "I'll just say I wouldn't put it past them to inject him with something and leave it there. Let's keep in mind that our witness is at an age when heart attacks are more common."

"True." It felt hollow, but what else was there to say?

"What about you? Are you still set on testifying?"

"Absolutely."

"Even though it's obvious you suspect the heart attack was cartel related?"

"Let me tell you something. The things I saw those scumbags do are seared into my memory. I want to take them down."

The women in the box truck being herded like cattle into waiting vans. Filthy, covered in bruises, looking like they hadn't eaten a decent meal in weeks. Chained together at the waist, one after another.

Not to mention the other items removed from the truck. Crates, one of which was opened to reveal plastic-wrapped bricks of white powder.

Brax had hidden himself in the shadows outside the warehouse—he'd been searching the riverbank for the presence of skid marks after a sketchy, staged car accident and happened to be around when the truck came through. Nobody had seen him in passing, and they hadn't noticed his presence outside the loading bay.

"They don't know who I am," he reminded the district attorney. "But I know who they are. I know who Prince Riviera is, and I've seen what he's capable of. No way I'm going to let this guy back out on the street. We both know he's the entire backbone of that organization. With him behind bars, they lose all their clout and protection. They'll go down in flames."

"You don't know how relieved I am to hear that. I was afraid the news would scare you off."

"I don't scare that easily, ma'am."

She chuckled this time, though it was short-lived. "Still, I want you to watch your back. There's no telling what these scumbags know. Let's not underestimate them."

Brax turned off the main road and onto the smaller, two-lane dirt road leading to his house. There it was, lit up inside, with two people waiting to welcome him home after a long day.

Now was not the time to underestimate anybody.

Chapter Ten

It had taken three days for Brax's friend to fix Tessa's phone. When Brax had come home Wednesday night, he'd presented it like a great treasure. "Here you go. Your key to freedom."

She couldn't help beaming at how happy it made him to provide her with a phone, even if she didn't quite understand the connection between it and her freedom.

Still, she'd accepted the gesture and thanked him profusely. "Not to be picky, but this isn't a car," she'd reminded him. "I'm not exactly free."

"Sure, you are. Don't I keep telling you to use my car? In fact..." His charming grin had widened, making him almost irresistible. "I took tomorrow off so you can go out. Do whatever it is you want to do."

Ice had formed in her stomach. "I can't do that. It's—"

"It's only fair to you," he'd insisted, kind but firm. He had that way about him. A gentleness that didn't seem to mix with his physical size and line of work.

"You've been working so hard. Two weeks without a break."

"It's nothing."

His brow had lowered. "Tessa, we both know I know what you go through with him. You might have more experience, but still. It's no cakewalk. Now that you have your phone back, we can both breathe a little easier. I know you didn't want to leave the house on your own without a phone handy."

"And you weren't crazy about the idea either."

"That's true." His smile had softened along with his voice. "Go out. Take care of yourself. Just for a day. You deserve it."

Which was what had led her to a mall in San Antonio. Even that morning, she'd resisted leaving the house until Brax had teased her, calling her "mother hen" since she was so worried about leaving Walker. *Mother.* The thought that he might know something had carried her out of the house in a blink. While he didn't seem like the type to play games, there was no telling. After all, Brax was related to Robert, the king of game players. She couldn't put anything past him.

For all her worrying, though, it felt good to walk through the mall. How long had it been since she'd taken the time to window shop? She couldn't remember the last time.

When she was a kid, the mall had been the place to hang out. Even then, however, older kids and her parents had talked about the way things used to be.

Back before online and big box store shopping had chipped away at mall culture.

There were a couple of groups of kids there in the late afternoon, long after school would've let out for the day. Otherwise, the only shoppers were older people. Some of them looked like they were getting exercise rather than paying any attention to store windows.

She paused at a baby store and smiled at a sweet nursery set, then studied a bouncy swing and wondered if it would be right for Walker. Granted, she didn't have the money for it—all of her money was stashed in her purse, every penny Brax had paid her up to this point minus the cost of a few necessities—but she might be able to talk him into it. Walker needed to build up his legs.

She knew Brax would deny him nothing. If he had his way, her son would grow up spoiled beyond all reason.

That didn't do anything to loosen the smile from her face. She caught sight of her reflection. She looked so happy.

All things considered, she didn't have any reason to be unhappy.

So what if she carried all her money around with her in case she needed to make a run for it?

So what if she still entertained the idea of running away with her baby from time to time? In the dark of night, lying in bed in Brax's guest room, sometimes that idea would sneak up on her. She couldn't get rid of it.

She stopped in front of a boutique to admire the mannequins in their spangly cocktail dresses. What would it be like to live the sort of life where she needed a dress like this? To get all fancied up and go out on the town?

On Brax's arm?

Another dangerous train of thought that also tended to visit her in the night.

She turned away from the window and checked her phone for the millionth time since leaving the house. No calls from Brax. Walker didn't need her.

She couldn't be separated from him again. Even a trip to the mall was too much time spent apart from her baby. Especially after what Robert had done.

Brax wasn't expecting her for at least another hour or two, but that didn't matter. She couldn't bear to be away from Walker for another minute.

It was getting dark by then. Time had slipped by while she'd wandered the mall. Was it possible for Walker to be afraid she'd left him—again? No, he was too young, wasn't he?

She wandered through a nearly empty parking lot and silently cursed herself for not parking under a light. Relieved to finally open the car door, something slammed into her from behind and sent her sprawling across the driver's side of Brax's car.

Not something. Someone.

Someone yanked her out of the car by her hair, pushed her against the door and pressed a gun against her back. "Quiet," a man rasped close to her ear, "or I'll blow a hole through you. You've already been more trouble than you're worth."

Bile rose in her throat. There was nobody to help her. Not a soul anywhere nearby.

"Where is Robert?"

"I don't know." She could barely hear herself, so she tried again. "I don't know where he is. I swear it."

"Where've you been for almost three weeks now? Is he out here? Is that why you came all this way?"

"I'm telling you. I don't have the first idea where he is. You're wasting your time."

That only earned her a jab in the back as he pressed the gun harder. "Where's the kid? You hiding him too?"

She swallowed against her rising horror, then gritted her teeth. How dare he even speak of her son?

"I have no idea what you're talking about. I don't know any kid." She turned her head just slightly, enough to make out part of the man's pockmarked face. "I'm telling you. Robert didn't exactly leave things on good terms between us. I might kill him myself if I ever see him again."

At least that part was true.

"Then who are you out here with? You ain't got no family. We know that much about you."

But they didn't know whether or not she was the mother of Robert's baby or where Walker was. They weren't as smart as they thought.

And they didn't know about Brax either. Otherwise, this thug would've mentioned him, if not by name, at least by description.

"It's none of your business. I already knew I made a mistake hooking up with Robert. I didn't know that mistake would haunt me this long." Also not a lie.

"Listen up." His body pressed her tighter against the car—the keys, wedged between her body and the door, dug into her ribs, but she didn't dare shift her weight or even breathe too deeply. "You better find out where Robert is and fast. We'll be watching you from now on, and we won't be so gentle next time."

He had her purse before she could think to react, shoving her against the car one last time. Her ribs screamed in protest as the breath left her lungs in a single rush and the world went slightly gray.

The squealing tires weren't loud enough to drown out the rush of blood in her ears.

Her purse. Her phone. All that money she'd been carrying around in case she needed to make a getaway. Everything she had in the world. Gone. Again.

But she was alive. And she had the car keys in her fist.

Once she was sure the other car was out of the lot, she opened the door and slid behind the wheel as gingerly as she could. Her ribs would hurt for a day or two, but that was fine compared to what might've happened.

"Breathe," she whispered, doing everything she could to drive normally. To not attract attention. It wouldn't do her any good to get pulled over when she'd just lost her license to a thug with a gun.

Somehow, she made it to the house without anyone following her there. With such light traffic, it would be difficult for anyone to follow her without being noticed. Another pair of headlights would stick out like a sore thumb, and no way could anybody drive that dirt road in the dark without flipping on their lights.

Her legs shook hard enough to send her tumbling into the house. Brax was by her side in an instant. "What's wrong? What happened?"

Was he holding her up? Yes, he was. She was in his arms, and he was holding her against him, and that was good. That was what she needed.

"My...my purse got stolen by some kids in the parking lot at the mall." Lies slid so easily out of her mouth nowadays.

"Are you okay? Did they hurt you?"

"Not really. One of them knocked me against the car, and I was dazed for a second. But that was it."

"How many were there? How old were they? Male, female?"

"Brax, please." She touched her forehead to his chest. "Let me breathe."

"Of course. I'm sorry." He held the back of her head in one hand, cradling it while his other arm held her close. "I'm so sorry that happened to you. You're safe now."

Safe. She barely managed to hold back a panicky laugh. There was no such thing as safe, not now. Maybe there never had been.

How could he keep her safe when she couldn't tell him the truth?

"I'll call some of my contacts with the San Antonio PD."

"No." She lifted her head. "Don't do that."

"Why not? They stole your purse, the little—"

"They're kids. I don't think what they did was okay, but let's face it. I doubt I'll ever get anything back at this point. I should've parked closer to the mall. I shouldn't have stayed so late when there was hardly anybody there."

"This isn't your fault. Don't blame yourself." He touched her cheek with the backs of his fingers, letting them glide down to her jaw. The tenderness of this gesture both eased her and stirred something deep inside her to life. "You're positive you aren't hurt?"

"I'm not hurt—and that's another reason to let this go. It isn't worth the time it would take for me to go to the station and fill out a report. I'll never see my purse again."

"You're still shaking." He guided her to the couch. "Sit. Rest. You've been through a lot."

He had no idea.

What would happen if they found her? Watched her? Saw her with Walker?

What about Brax? What would they do to him if he tried to help her?

"It's been a stressful evening so far." She slid the elastic from her hair and shook it out over her shoulders, scrubbing her fingers into her scalp. What was she supposed to do now? She didn't even have her escape money. Nothing to support Walker with.

"It's been a stressful couple of weeks." Brax sat beside her, close enough for their legs to touch. She would normally have moved away out of reflex, but not now. Not when she needed the comfort of his nearness.

"It has, I guess. But I love it," she insisted, looking at him in mixed earnestness and panic. What was he leading up to? "I love being with Walker. I'm happy here."

"You need to step back, though. I've put too much in your hands. You're here alone all day. It would get to anybody."

It was a sick joke. Here he was, concerned for her and completely missing the mark. This sweet, caring, generous man.

And all she could do was lie.

"Tomorrow's Friday," he mused. "Why don't you take the weekend off? I don't have anything pressing to manage. I could take Walker to meet my parents, and you can have the whole weekend to yourself. Think of it as a mini-vacation. Treat yourself. Go stay with some friends."

She bit back a hysterical laugh. *What friends?*

"I'll borrow one of my brothers' cars for the weekend, and you can take mine. If you get ticketed for driving without a license, call me and I'll use one of the favors the San Antonio PD owes me to get you out of it." He stood, smiling like it was all settled. "I should finish making dinner. I'm not half the cook you are, but you've inspired me to break out the pots and pans."

How was she supposed to say no? She had no legitimate reason to. He didn't know she'd lost every cent she had to her name—he thought she had a bank account, for heaven's sake, and that she'd been depositing the generous amounts of cash he paid.

There was no fighting it. She had no reason to say no unless she felt like confessing the entire truth. That wasn't going to happen.

"Okay." She shrugged with a sinking heart. "Sounds great."

Chapter Eleven

"You sure I can't get you something to eat?"

Tessa felt sorry for the waitress. The poor woman was only trying to earn a decent tip, or at least to turn over the table in hopes that the next customer to sit there would order a meal and leave a few bucks.

She offered an apologetic smile. "Just coffee for me. Thank you." The waitress frowned before walking away.

Tessa wanted to spill her guts, to put it all out there. How hungry she was. How the aroma of fried food and juicy burgers made her mouth water and her empty stomach clench up tight.

How almost every cent she had in the world was going to this endless cup of coffee, which at least she could get free refills on. It helped curb her appetite, though not by much.

And being inside the diner gave her someplace warm, dry and safe to while away the hours.

What a fun Friday night she was having.

Looking around, she was reminded of the world still turning. There were people whose lives made sense. People who went out on a Friday night, had fun and went to the diner for a plate of fries or a stack of pancakes to soak up the alcohol they'd just drank. People who got together with friends and talked about their week before comparing weekend plans.

Life went on for these people. They didn't know what it meant to live one lie after another. What it was like to feel her desperation. Forced to spend endless hours alone with nowhere to go, all so she could be with her baby. So his guardian wouldn't know about the lies Robert had concocted.

She wasn't the first person to deal with this, and she knew it. Being homeless, having no money.

Which was probably the only thing that kept her going. Knowing other people also dealt with challenges.

She chuckled at the sight of the purse sitting next to her in the booth. Brax had been so happy when he'd gotten the call that morning from her cell—somebody had turned it in at the police station after finding it in the mall parking lot. It hadn't gotten far after all.

Even her phone and wallet were still inside. Her driver's license, all of it.

Except for the money.

Just another cruel joke. Having to pretend to be happy her purse had been found. Brax didn't know she'd carried all of her money inside. And there was no way of telling him without revealing a whole lot more.

So even though she'd been terrified at the thought

of losing Walker for the weekend and distraught at knowing she had no money, she'd marveled over how smart it had been for the officer to call the most recent contact in her cell and ask if they knew her. How lucky she was to have her wallet and phone back.

Right. Lucky.

It was easy to fall into despair, especially when she had the prospect of spending the night in the back seat of Brax's car to look forward to. Though all things considered, it was better than an alley.

A flash of light reflecting off metal caught her eye, made her look out the window. Pure reflex, nothing more than that.

Reflex fast enough that she was able to catch sight of a pockmarked face staring out from inside a car passing slowly outside.

She knew that face. She'd never forget it. Just like she'd never forget the sound of his voice as he'd warned her to find Robert.

What was she supposed to do? She was trapped, cornered, her heart thudding. The car rounded the block but would be back. She knew it in her bones.

Her hands shook as she dug around for the loose change she'd collected—she wouldn't stiff her waitress, even now.

The sight of her phone sitting there in the bag froze her in place.

Her phone. This confirmed that was how they kept finding her. Whenever she left it on, somebody came sniffing around. It was how they'd tracked her to the office building, how her attacker had found her at the mall.

Now, how he'd found her at the diner.

She dropped a handful of quarters on the table before ducking into the ladies' room, careful to keep her head down, her face turned away from the window in case the car came around again. She fought the impulse to run, struggled to remain calm, to act as if nothing out of the ordinary was going on.

Once she was inside with the door locked, she looked around. No, the windows were too narrow. No escape through there.

With a deep breath and a silent prayer, she erased the contacts in her phone—she couldn't leave Brax vulnerable—before leaving it lying on the counter and ducking out of the room.

It wasn't easy, cutting her last tie to the rest of the world, and it would be hard to explain how she lost it again. But whatever it took to make Brax believe her, she would do.

She kept her head down, taking the exit closest to the restroom rather than the main door out front. It was dark, almost eleven o'clock, with plenty of cars in the lot to hide behind.

The car pulled up near the door she'd just come out of. An older model, a little banged up. Professional villainy must not pay much, she guessed.

A few panic-filled minutes later, the passenger went inside. She could barely see over the hood of the car she'd hidden behind, crouching in weeds and broken glass. The pockmarked driver stayed behind the wheel, peering out over the lot.

She hardly dared breathe, much less move. Could he see her? Did he know she was there?

After a few minutes, the man came out from the diner and muttered something to the driver before getting back into the car and slamming the door. He was angry. They both were. Their voices carried her way, faint but audible. Plenty of unsavory words were thrown around.

Brax's car was only four down from the car she hid behind. The only real shot she had of getting away was putting as much distance between those two buffoons and herself as possible. As soon as they left, she'd have to get out of there.

She moved slowly, carefully, one eye always on her pursuers. They were arguing over what to do next, she guessed, too busy to notice any movement up ahead.

Or to notice Brax's car parked right in front of them. It was the same car she'd used at the mall, so one would think they'd stake it out until she appeared. They must not have considered it. Too busy wondering why they couldn't pin her down.

The driver pulled away—slowly, cautiously, like he was waiting for her to pop out from the shadows at any second. He wasn't a complete idiot. But he couldn't stay there all night, idling in the lot and blocking cars from leaving or entering.

She crept alongside the door and opened it just enough to slide inside, closing it quickly to kill the interior light. Her pursuers were gone. There was nobody to see.

That didn't mean she was out of danger, and she knew it.

Seatbelt fastened, hands at the perfect ten and two on the wheel—which she was practically crushing with her grip—she eased out of the lot and started driving.

But where could she go?

She certainly couldn't spend the entire night driving. There was only so much gas in the tank, and she had no money to refill it.

A deep, head-splitting yawn answered any further questions. She'd been up since five with Walker, and it was now half past eleven. Even a gallon of coffee couldn't combat her deep fatigue.

She eyed the parking lot of a supermarket. Would it be a good place to pull into and go to sleep?

Before she could make a decision, a flash of headlights in the mirror almost blinded her. She turned her head away, blinking hard. Some people were such jerks. There was no reason to follow so—

Her already cramping hands gripped the wheel harder as that familiar tingling sensation prickled at the back of her neck.

A sudden right turn pointed her in the direction of downtown. The car behind her took a right too.

He'd only gone around the block again.

Tears threatened to spill onto her cheeks. She couldn't let them. Wouldn't. It would mean she was beaten, but she hadn't been beaten yet.

The cars and cabs and pedestrians of a downtown Friday night were just what she needed. Not that she expected to blend in, but tailing her would be more of a challenge with so many obstacles to get around. As it was, groups of people crossed in the middle of the street, not bothering to walk to the corner. Cars double-parked to drop off and pick up. It took time just to creep from one light to the next.

Tessa steered around one of those double-parked cars and was glad to see the double-parker pulled out before her pursuers could get past. The pockmarked man leaned on the horn, shouting something that blended in with the noise of the street.

She took advantage of this and made a sharp left at the next corner, barely missing a couple who'd started to cross without seeing her. She winced, waving in apology before flooring the gas pedal, then took another left at the next corner.

Right, left. Doubling back on herself. Always checking in the mirror. She'd thought she'd caught a glimpse of her tail now and then, but never for long. There were too many people in the way, too many cars suddenly pulling out of spaces and blocking the view.

After an hour of playing cat and mouse with Robert's *friends*, Tessa was fairly confident she'd lost them for good. Her vision was starting to blur, and real, true exhaustion set in once the adrenaline rush calmed down.

She pulled in behind a dark strip mall. Another

alley. She sensed a pattern, but at least nobody would come looking for her behind the row of stores.

And if they did, she mused as she stretched out along the back seat, she was too tired to make another successful getaway.

"WHAT ARE YOU doing up?"

Brax stopped walking halfway down the stairs at the sound of his mother's voice. She wasn't the only person in the kitchen. Both Sheila and Clinton Patterson were up and around at four in the morning.

He found them sitting at the table, both reading a newspaper that had to still be hot off the press. Coffee was brewing in a pot.

"Well?" Sheila asked, eyeing him from over the top of a page.

"I couldn't sleep." He pointed from one of them to the other. "And you two? Is this the norm?"

"We're both early birds, you know that." Clinton set down the section he'd been reading and picked up another.

"But four o'clock?"

They exchanged a look. "Well, we were hoping to be up when the baby wakes. You said he gets up before dawn."

"I should've known." Brax snickered, taking a seat at the table. "You're incorrigible."

But it meant the world to him. Watching his parents fall in love with his nephew. They'd taken the news in stride—neither of them had a great opinion of Robert, so the news of him skipping town and handing guardianship over hadn't shocked them much.

It only made sense for him to bring Walker to meet them. After all, they were the people who'd taught Brax what it meant to be part of a family.

"What kept you from sleeping?" Sheila leaned in with a motherly expression, otherwise known as *scrutiny*. "I don't like those circles under your eyes."

"Thanks." He leaned back in his chair with a shrug and remembered being a kid. New to the entire concept of family. Resenting the questions his foster mother asked.

He wasn't that kid anymore.

Which was what made him sit up straight. "I kept worrying about the woman who takes care of Walker while I'm at work."

"Tessa, right?" Clinton asked, lowering the paper. "You mentioned her."

"Right. She's young, and she strikes me as being... wounded somehow. I wish I could explain it. She's troubled. Jumpy sometimes. She never offers any information about herself other than having taken care of Walker for a little while back in Eagle Pass. I gave her the weekend off to take care of herself since she's been with Walker twenty-four seven for two weeks straight. She deserved it."

"You said she stays with you?" his dad asked.

"Yes."

"So she's at the house now? Why not call her?"

"For one thing, it's not even dawn yet. She's probably asleep. For another, no, she's not at the house. I don't know where she went. She didn't share her plans."

Sheila cocked her head to the side. Brax knew that move. It meant he was in trouble.

"When did you give her this gift of free time?"

"Thursday night. I told her I'd taken the weekend off and she should do the same."

"And you forced her out of the house? Two weeks after forcing her to move in with you?"

"I didn't force her to do anything, Mom."

Clinton cleared his throat. "What your mother is trying to say is, you gave that poor girl nowhere to go. What if she didn't have much money saved up? Not everybody can book a hotel room at the last minute. No wonder you're worried about her. Your subconscious is nagging you."

"You said she's secretive and jumpy," Sheila added. "What if you're her only means of safety right now? She couldn't have been living a safe, steady sort of life if she was able to pick up and move into your spare bedroom at a moment's notice. You could be the godsend she was waiting for."

"Oh, no." He held his head in his hands. Why hadn't he seen it sooner? "I should've thought about that. It's obvious she's been hiding something. She looked so fragile and alone when I first met her."

"Give her a call," Clinton suggested. "If you're worried enough about her that it kept you up all night, call her."

"It's too early."

"Call her anyway. You can ease your worries, and she'll know you were thinking about her. You can't lose."

Strange. It was like he'd been waiting for permission. The second he knew his parents thought it would be okay for him to call, he was up from the table and going out to the living room for a little privacy.

Tessa would forgive him for waking her up, wouldn't she?

"Where are you, bitch?"

Like he'd been slapped, Brax's head snapped back at the sound of the snarl that greeted him.

"What, you calling to see if we found your phone? Well, we did, you sneaky—"

"Who is this?" Brax barked, cutting the man off before he could insult Tessa again.

There was silence. Then, "Who's this?"

"I asked first. Who has this phone? Who are you? Where are you?" From the corner of his eye, he caught sight of his parents entering the room. His mom held her hands over her mouth.

More silence. Then a beep to signal the call's end.

"What was that about?" Clinton asked.

"I have no idea. But some foul-mouthed bully has Tessa's phone." He called the number again, but this time it rang endlessly with no answer.

Memories of Thursday night hit him from all sides.

She'd been so shaken up—maybe too shaky for her purse to have been stolen by kids.

Did this have to do with whoever had mugged her at the mall?

He ran up to his room without further explanation and went straight to the laptop he'd left on the nightstand. Tessa was driving his car while he'd borrowed Chance's Jeep. All of their cars had GPS installed so they could track mileage as a tax deduction.

"Oh, you've got to be kidding me." The sight of Tessa's erratic driving patterns from just a few short hours ago made his stomach churn. Why had she been going up and down one street after another in the downtown section? Why had she spent a solid hour doubling back over herself?

And why was the car now parked at some strip mall?

Who was she meeting?

Or, worse, who'd stolen the car? What had happened to her?

One thing was clear: Tessa was in trouble.

He pulled on his clothes and headed downstairs again, where his parents waited. "Can you keep watch over Walker for a little while? I have to find her. There's trouble."

"Of course. Help her," Sheila urged.

He intended to do just that.

Chapter Twelve

Brax cursed himself the entire way to the location where Tessa had parked his car.

What had he been thinking? Had he thought at all?

It didn't seem that way, looking at the situation through new eyes. Now that his mom had set him straight, he couldn't believe he'd thought he was being the good guy by practically forcing Tessa out of the house for the weekend.

He didn't know the first thing about her. Not really. Nothing substantial. Only that she loved Walker. At least they agreed about that.

Otherwise? He'd imagined her going to a hotel, maybe getting a manicure or whatever young women did when they wanted to pamper themselves. A facial, a haircut. It wasn't like he knew a lot about those things.

Now, he tried to imagine the situation through the eyes of a woman with nowhere else to go.

But why didn't she have any other options? That was the question. He had nothing but questions about her.

She was behind a strip mall. He rounded the corner of the store on the end and instantly made out the shape of his car parked in the shadows of a line of trees behind the loading area.

And the sight of another car swinging into view at the opposite end of the mall, headlights washing over the glass-strewn concrete. It was barely dawn. What were they doing there?

It was clear soon enough as the car stopped and two men jumped out and headed straight for his car, marching with fisted hands swinging at their sides.

Brax acted before he thought, flooring the gas pedal, tires squealing as he raced their way. His approach startled them both into stopping.

"What are you doing?" he demanded on rushing out of the Jeep. "Get out of here."

One of them snorted. "Get lost, boy scout."

"I don't know who you're looking at, but I'm well past the age of being a boy scout." When the second man continued toward the car, even trying to open one of the doors, he shouted, "I said, leave it alone."

"Who the hell are you?"

"I'm the guy whose car you're touching, and you might want to take your hands off it right damn now." Brax didn't raise his voice.

Suddenly, so suddenly all three of them jumped in surprise, the door swung open and out popped Tessa.

Brax didn't have time to figure out the implications of this—Had she slept in the car? Why?—before he caught sight of what she held in one hand.

The bat he'd forgotten he'd left in the back seat.

"Get in the Jeep!" he shouted, moving forward to

put himself between Tessa and the men now stalking toward her.

One of the men shoved him, or tried to, and was visibly surprised when Brax didn't budge. And even more surprised when Brax's fist crashed into his jaw and sent him falling back.

Tessa grunted. Brax turned to her, ready to kill whoever had put their hands on her, but found that she'd grunted in the act of swinging the bat and it connecting with the second man.

"He was going to jump you from behind," she gasped, looking down at the man who'd collapsed with both hands against his lower back.

Brax didn't waste time waiting for the guys to recover. He took her hand, running for the Jeep. She jumped inside and within moments, they'd fled the lot.

"They'll follow us." She sounded so confident. And so flat. Matter-of-fact.

"I trust they will." It was the Riviera cartel. It had to be. They'd been searching for his car.

And he might've gotten her killed.

She turned in the seat, peering behind them. "Yeah, I see a car coming out of the parking lot. Turn as soon as you can. They might not see us yet, especially if they're both dazed."

"They'll be dazed and furious," he grunted, knowing the lengths men like that would go to make somebody pay for hurting them. He took a quick right, tires squealing, and thanked his lucky stars there weren't many cars on the road at this time of the morning.

She faced forward again. "Maybe that little side street," she suggested, pointing up ahead. How was she still so calm? Was she in shock?

She should've been screaming. Demanding answers. If he hadn't gotten there when he had...

He turned onto the side street and cruised a little more slowly. They were now in a residential area. The last thing he wanted was to strike an innocent bystander out for their morning jog.

Tessa looked behind them again. "I think they just turned onto the street three blocks back. I can't really make out the car."

"Okay." He took a left, then another quick left, before making a right, which led back to the commercial area. There was a road ahead that he knew led out of town.

"How did you know where to find me?" she asked, still looking behind them.

"I wasn't sure I'd find you there. I was looking for my car."

"Why?"

Guilt raced through him. She'd really flip her lid now. Bracing himself, he explained, "I was worried, so I tracked the car's GPS. I tried calling you earlier, but a man picked up and shouted at me. Did you lose your phone?"

"I left it at a diner."

He waited for more explanation. She didn't offer one.

"Okay." He drew out the word. What was she trying to get at? Why would she leave her phone behind?

That choice of words too. She'd left it. She didn't lose it. She didn't forget it. She'd performed a deliberate act. And it didn't seem to come as a shock that he'd tracked her. Like she didn't care.

Why?

"Wait." She clutched his shoulder. Now he was in for it. This was where she'd lose it on him. "Where's Walker?"

"He's fine. He's with my parents." She let out a sigh that sounded a lot like relief before letting go of him. Was that all she cared about?

Not the fact that two men had almost attacked her?

"I'm so sorry." He checked the mirror for signs of them on his tail. "This is all my fault. I've put you in danger. It's unforgivable."

She didn't reply. It had to be shock. No wonder. She'd been through something that had probably traumatized her.

He had done this to her.

After an hour of driving aimlessly, erratic turns and more than a few blown stoplights, Brax was positive they'd lost their tail. Tessa sat upright, unable or unwilling to relax.

"I think we're safe. Let's go back to my parents' house for now. We'll figure out what to do when we get there."

"Okay."

He glanced over and found her checking the mirrors. Still watching.

Seeing her like that was the final nail in the coffin. He knew what he had to do. There was no excuse for dragging her into his problems, for ruining her life, for putting her through this.

"Tessa, I have to tell you this. You can't work for me anymore." It was one of the hardest things he'd ever forced himself to say.

He didn't want it this way. In fact, now that he'd said it, he knew just how much he wanted the opposite. For her to stay. To be part of his life. But she didn't deserve to be hunted and attacked. Having her in his life was too risky. Her safety mattered more than his feelings for her.

She made a sound that seemed almost like a wounded animal. "No, please. I can't… I can't…"

"I'm sorry. You can't understand how much I hate this."

"But…no. Please. I need…"

He scrubbed a hand down his face. She was scared of losing her income. "Hey, don't worry. I'll give you another two weeks' salary to hold you over until you find another job. Can you find a place to stay? I'll help you with that too."

He glanced over at her. She was shaking, wrapping her arms around her middle like she might fly apart. Her eyes were darting around the Jeep. "What did I do wrong? Why are you sending me away?"

He recognized a panic attack when he saw one and sped up. "Tessa, you have to breathe. We'll get you through this. Don't panic."

"Don't panic?" She laughed—bitter, jagged—then sucked in a breath. "I can't leave you and Walker!

Don't make me, please. I'll do whatever you want, I swear. Don't make me leave."

"This is for your safety."

Her arms wrapped tighter around herself. She was rocking back and forth. "Please let me stay. Please."

By the time he pulled up in front of his parents' house, she was almost hysterical, shaking from the force of her emotions. Some of this had to be residual from this morning, but he couldn't add to it.

"Hey." He reached out, touching her shoulder. "Hey, it's going to be okay. If you really want to stay, you can."

She nodded over and over. "I do. Thank you."

She was thanking *him*? He was just hoping he wasn't about to put her in danger again.

He offered her a smile that started out forced but became genuine once he saw her palpable relief. And he couldn't deny the relief he felt in turn. He hadn't wanted Tessa to leave, even if it was for her own safety.

Now all that was left was figuring out how to move forward.

Chapter Thirteen

Tessa opened her eyes slowly. Why were they so heavy? It would be better to go back to sleep. She was so comfortable...

It all rushed back at once before sleep could overtake her again.

The fight in the parking lot. The zigzagging around trying to lose the men following them. Doing the same thing by herself, terrified, unable to call anybody for help.

Her eyes opened fully, and she looked around. Where was she?

The hazy memory of Brax leading her into the house came back in pieces. Only once she'd seen Walker for herself did she let Brax put her to bed. Everything was blank after that.

She'd had a breakdown. The memory made her wince in embarrassment. He had to think she was off her rocker. She couldn't help it, though, not when he'd told her she had to go. The idea of being kept away from Walker again was too much.

It had broken her. Combined with the fear and exhaustion, she had lost her grip. There'd been nothing left in her.

Now, she had to find a way to look him in the eye. It was humiliating.

He would have questions. Although for some reason, it was as if he blamed himself for those goons coming after her. Why would he think that? Now that she could think clearly, it was obvious he'd told her to look for another job because he thought it was for the best. Hadn't he mentioned her safety?

Or was that just an excuse to get rid of her?

Judging by the amber light coming through the window, she'd slept most of the day away. Great, now his entire family would think she was a crackpot or a druggie like Robert had claimed.

Humiliating or not, she had to get out of bed and face the consequences of her actions.

After freshening up in the hall bathroom, she crept downstairs. There were voices in the kitchen, one of which was Brax's. Would he hate her? Or— and this was somehow worse—pity her?

"Hey, look who's up," Brax greeted her with a smile. He slid out the chair next to him at the long table. "How are you feeling?"

"Better now that I've slept, thanks."

What mattered more than anything, what her eyes kept darting over to look at, was her son. He was in the arms of a beautiful woman with a warm smile. Even when Walker took a fistful of her dark hair and pulled, she only laughed indulgently.

"Tessa? I'm Clinton Patterson." Brax's dad. His

large hand engulfed hers. "And this is my wife, Sheila."

"I'm glad to meet you. Thank you for letting me sleep here for a little while. I was—"

"Think nothing of it." There wasn't so much as a hint of anything but pure kindness in Sheila's voice, in her expression. "I'm glad to see you looking better. We were worried about you when you first got here. You looked worn out."

That was an understatement.

Walker burst out with a string of very forceful babble, making them all laugh. "This one's going to have a lot to say once he learns to talk, isn't he?" Clinton leaned over him, making funny faces, and Walker giggled before taking one of the man's fingers in his fist.

"What a grip!" Clinton gasped in mock surprise, which made Walker giggle again.

They were sweet people, but then she'd figured that out already. The sort of people with room in their hearts for children in need of love. Watching them take to Walker the way they did was a beautiful thing.

Though pretending she didn't ache to hold him wasn't exactly easy.

Clinton turned to Brax. "While I have you here, can you help me move some boxes in the garage?"

"Sure." Brax glanced at Tessa like he was wary of leaving her alone with his mom. She did her best not to look too nervous.

It helped that Walker seemed so happy. Sheila

bounced him on her hip with a grin that almost touched her ears. "He's such a sweetheart."

"He is," Tessa agreed. She folded her arms across her chest to keep from reaching for him. It was torture not being able to hold him after everything she'd gone through in the past twenty-four hours.

"I'm about to get dinner started." Sheila appeared to study Tessa, arching an eyebrow. "Can you hold him for me while I cook?"

"Yes, of course." It was nothing less than a gift. She held out her arms and gratefully accepted her baby, hugging him tight and kissing his forehead. "Hey, buddy. I missed you."

"It's nice to have a baby around." Sheila got to work chopping vegetables. "So, tell me about yourself. Brax says you've been a miracle. I guess you can understand how unprepared he was."

She sensed Walker's honorary grandmother was giving her the third degree, but at least Sheila was kind and gentle about it.

"There isn't much to tell," Tessa admitted. "My parents died in a car accident two years ago. I've been on my own since then."

"Oh, I'm so sorry." It wasn't mere lip service. Sincerity poured from her.

"It sort of derailed my plans," she continued. "You know, college and all that. I had to focus on supporting myself."

"Naturally." Sheila glanced up from the cutting board. "So, you're a nanny now?"

"Right. I love it. I love being around kids." One in particular, whose head she kissed again.

"I know the feeling. It's part of the reason my husband and I decided to adopt. That, and we shared a desire to provide what children were missing. Like Brax, for example."

Tessa listened harder. She couldn't help it.

"He's a charmer, my son," Sheila chuckled before blowing a whistle between pursed lips. "He could charm the birds from the trees, that one. Always quick with a smile or a joke. Very clever too. Many's the time I wished he wasn't half so clever."

Tessa grinned. "I bet."

"But it could've turned out much differently." Sheila wasn't joking anymore. Her brows drew together. "He was alone for most of his childhood. Neglected. Very poor. It seems to me he remembers that experience and the memories are what make him determined to help others. He's protective of people in similar situations. All alone, fending for themselves."

"I see."

"I would hate to see anybody take advantage of that."

They exchanged a look that spoke volumes, said more than words ever could. "I would hate that too," Tessa murmured.

"I thought you would." Sheila wiped her hands on her apron before going to the fridge. "He was a tough nut to crack, even though it might be hard to imagine now. It took a while to get through to him. He held a lot of secrets he wasn't ready to share. That's a heavy burden for anyone to carry."

The woman's back was to her, half-bent while looking through the fridge, so Tessa couldn't see her face. How much did she know? Why was she conveniently talking about secrets?

What had Brax told her?

It couldn't have been anything too bad, since Sheila was smiling when she turned back toward Tessa and Walker. "It's important to trust people, I think. Good people. Brax is a good man—all of my sons are. They've helped so many. It seems they have a limitless capacity for compassion and service."

"And they have you to thank for that."

"I can't take all the credit. My husband had a hand in it too."

"Hey." Brax joined them a moment later, looking between the women like he was trying to decide if everything was okay. "How's it going in here?"

"Oh, you know. Just chatting while Walker does his darndest to understand what we're saying." Sheila beamed at Walker, who waved his fists.

Brax touched Tessa's back. "We'd better get moving."

Sheila sighed. "I was fixing dinner for you!"

"Sorry. I need to talk to the others about what happened this morning and I have to pick up my car. Chance would probably like his Jeep back at some point." He looked to Tessa with a sheepish shrug. "I'm sorry."

"You don't owe me an apology." They got Walker's things together and said goodbye to the Pattersons.

"I expect to see you both again, and soon." Sheila hugged Tessa before letting her out the door, then kissed Walker's chubby cheeks. "I could just eat him up."

"Not if I do it first." They laughed together before Tessa followed Brax to the Jeep.

Inside the Jeep was a different story. There was no laughter.

In fact, Brax looked downright murderous. "I have to tell you something I should've told you way before now. I never imagined it would seep into my personal life."

"What is it?"

"I'm testifying in a few days against the Riviera cartel. I don't know if you've ever heard of them."

"I'd have to be living under a rock to never hear the name."

"Yeah, well, it looks like they already put one of the two witnesses out of commission. I don't know whether the heart attack he had was natural or induced. Either way, it looks like they're coming after me now. I was so confident they didn't know who I was, but what other explanation is there?"

Silence hung heavy between them as Tessa struggled to process this. "You…think what happened this morning was related to the cartel trouble?"

"They found my car. Why else would they be looking for it? That's why I wanted to let you go.

I didn't want you to suffer over this again. You've been through enough because of me."

On one hand, her heart swelled at the thought of him caring that much about her. Wanting to keep her out of harm's way.

On the other hand, she just about wanted to melt away under the weight of her guilt. He thought he was the reason she was being stalked.

Sheila's comment about the burden of secrets rang out in Tessa's memory. That was no random piece of wisdom—she'd known it at the time too. Sheila Patterson was a mother through and through, dropping little bits of advice without coming right out with the unvarnished facts.

There was nothing left to do but tell the truth. She owed it to Brax.

She owed it to her son.

What if he takes Walker away? The question made her shiver. The fact was, unless they played it safe from now on, one of the goons looking for Robert might kidnap Walker to get to him. More than likely Robert wouldn't care. He'd be too concerned about his own life to worry about his son's.

But those creeps wouldn't know that, would they?

Walker's safety meant more than anything.

So much, in fact, that Tessa cleared her throat. "There's something you need to know. I should've told you from the beginning, but I was too afraid."

"Afraid? Of what?" He didn't sound surprised, she noticed. He'd always treated her like he was waiting for her to come clean about something or other. Like he would accept her explanations even if he didn't actually believe them.

The phone rang before she could continue. Brax touched a button on the steering wheel to answer. "Hello?"

"It's Weston." He didn't sound happy. "Is Tessa with you?"

"Yeah, she's right here." Brax glanced her way.

She couldn't breathe.

"I'm sorry to tell you this," Weston continued, "but she isn't who she says she is. You need to be careful."

Chapter Fourteen

"Weston? I think you should know you're on speaker." Brax looked to Tessa for some sign. Some surprise or shock. Something.

She sat still, staring straight ahead. The only thing to give away the strain she was under was the way she clenched her fists in her lap.

"Do you want me to call back later? When you're alone?"

"Don't bother." Tessa's voice was heavy with... defeat? Fatigue? "Go ahead."

"What's going on?" Brax demanded. It didn't matter which of them thought the question was directed their way.

Weston sighed heavily. "I found Walker's birth certificate. According to this, his mother's name is Theresa Mahoney."

It was a good thing Brax was pulling down the road, just in front of the house. He might've gotten them in an accident otherwise. As it was, he felt like he'd just been run over by an eighteen-wheeler.

Walker's mother wasn't dead. *Tessa* was his mother.

He pulled to a stop and put the Jeep into Park but didn't bother opening the door. Neither did she. Walker slept in the back, blissfully unaware.

"Tessa's parental rights were stripped," Weston continued. "Due to drug use. And, of course, she's never worked for a nanny service. She tricked us."

It got worse with every passing second.

Brax looked to her for something, anything. Explanation. Anger. Instead, there she was, slumped against the door like she wanted to melt into it. If that wasn't an admission of guilt, he didn't know what was.

"I'm sorry to break it to you like this. But I thought you needed to know."

It took a second for Brax to find his voice. "Thanks. I'll call you later."

The silence was unbearable. Heavy, thick, making it hard to breathe. For someone who'd been able to come up with quick responses and charming phrases all his life, being left with nothing to say was a new experience.

"Is there a reason I didn't hear about this from you?" he finally asked.

"I didn't know if you'd want to listen." She ran a hand under both eyes.

"You'd better believe I want to hear your side of this after you've lied all these weeks."

"What was I supposed to do?" She whirled on him. Instead of screaming, her voice fell into a hissing whisper, which was somehow more effective than the shrillest shriek.

"Yes, I'm Walker's mother. And the reason I came to you was because I had nowhere else to go. The day you called about Walker, that first day, I got home from work and found my apartment ransacked. They stole my money and threatened to beat me up. All because they were looking for Robert and figured I knew where to find him."

"Did you?"

"He took our son away from me because he's a spiteful, hateful monster. Why would he tell me anything about his plans?" She snorted. "He dropped me the minute he got what he wanted."

So far that sounded like Robert.

She looked into the back seat, and her gaze softened a little. "I had nowhere else to go. I didn't even know you had Walker until you called. Robert took him away."

"You had nothing to do with that?"

Her head snapped around again, and he wished he hadn't said it. "You know your brother. Do you think he's beyond setting me up?"

"Did he?"

She raised an eyebrow. "I've lived with you for more than two weeks. Have I ever given you even the slightest indication I had a drug problem?"

"You could've gotten yourself clean by now."

He had never seen so much disdain packed into a single eye roll. "Fine. But it isn't true. What Robert said isn't true at all. He set me up, lied about me and he took Walker away. Why he would do that when he was only going to hand him over to you, I have no idea. I've never been able to understand him."

That made two of them.

"How did you get involved with him in the first place?"

She shrugged with a sigh. "I was a cocktail waitress at a casino in Eagle Pass. He was in there a lot. Charming. Handsome. I had just lost my parents not long before that and was on my own. Lonely." Another quick hand under her eyes.

Brax bit back his sympathy in favor of letting her talk. Hadn't he wanted to know the truth about her all this time?

"Maybe a week after we slept together, Robert stopped calling. Looking back, I realize I shouldn't have been surprised. He didn't care about me. But I was hurt and angry. Then I found out I was pregnant. I managed to get hold of him. He told me the baby couldn't be his because he'd used protection. So I was on my own again."

"I have to ask." Damn it. This was a hard question. "Are you sure Walker is his—"

"He was the only one," she snapped.

"Okay."

"If he wasn't going to help me I decided I would make it on my own. I worked hard. Took extra shifts. Started cleaning houses on the side to make extra money."

"While pregnant?"

"I had to support the baby somehow, didn't I? But it was okay. I guess it felt like I had a purpose again. A direction. Without my parents, I'd lost my way. Nothing bad, but I was drifting. I stopped taking my college classes, stopped seeing friends. With the baby to work for, there was a reason to get out of bed every morning."

She looked down at her hands. "Robert showed up at the hospital when Walker was born. Said he was sorry and that he wanted to be part of our lives. I was stupid enough to believe him. He even stuck around my apartment for the first two weeks. I told myself he wasn't as helpful as he could've been because he didn't know anything about babies. But there were other things that weren't so easy to explain away. Like the way he kept peeking out the window from behind the curtains."

"I have a feeling I know where this is going."

"He got a call after two weeks. I don't know who it was from, but it was enough to get him to pack up his things and tell me he was only using me and Walker as a way to hide out. He didn't really want to be a father. I shouldn't expect to see him again."

Brax winced. He could almost see it playing out in his head.

"It was okay, though. There was another single mom in my building who worked during the day shift. I watched her little girl along with Walker while she was working, and she watched Walker for me at night so I could work."

"You must've been exhausted."

"Yeah." She sighed. "But we were making it. I could pay the rent, keep him in diapers and get formula and clothes, feed myself. It was hard, but it was good. He was worth it."

Another heavy sigh. "Robert came back when Walker was almost two months old, and said he wanted to be part of our lives again. This time I told him to get lost."

"Good for you."

"It wasn't good enough for him, though. I know that now. A couple of days later, I was leaving the casino when a man bumped into me. That's all I remember. He bumped into me, and everything got blurry. Somehow I made it home, but I was fuzzy and my coordination was all off. When CPS showed up, I was completely unable to pull it together."

Her breathing picked up speed. "They took Walker away. Pulled him out of my arms. He was screaming. I knew in my head that I had to do something, but I couldn't understand anything coming out of my mouth no matter how hard I tried to make sense. All I remember is them saying somebody reported me for neglect and drug use. It was a nightmare. The sort of thing you see in a movie. It kept getting worse. Robert made it look like the whole 'being on drugs' thing was the norm. I know now that whoever bumped into me must've injected something, but I couldn't prove it. I couldn't prove I was a good mother. He got a judge to permanently revoke my parental rights."

She snorted. "I didn't have any money or any way to prove I was innocent. I didn't know what to do."

Walker stirred and fussed. It gave Brax an excuse

to get out of the car. Sitting there wondering what to believe—whether it was right or wrong to take what he knew about Robert and allow himself to believe his brother would go that far—would drive him crazy before long.

He unstrapped Walker and held him against his shoulder. Tessa got out on her side. "Do you believe me or not?"

"I don't know."

She shook her head, color bleeding from her face. "You think I'd make up something like this?"

Brax faced her in front of the Jeep. "Do I think Robert would stoop to anything? Yes. Do I believe he'd completely make up something like this? It's hard. Why would he even want a baby?"

Tessa's eyes filled with tears. And he realized how unbelievably stupid it was not to believe her. Playing it smart and exercising caution were one thing. But this was a woman with nothing to lose because she'd already lost everything.

And she loved Walker. *That* Brax could have zero doubt about.

"I don't think you'd make this up," he had to admit. "I believe Robert would sink to any level to get what he wanted. I couldn't have guessed he would ever stoop this low, though. I'm sorry he did that to you."

"Thank you."

"That doesn't mean I'm not furious with you for lying the way you did. For weeks. Every time I asked you about yourself. Every time I commented on how good you were with him. You pretended to be a nanny. You—"

"I didn't know how you would react." Her tears spilled over. She didn't brush them away this time. "I figured you would take Walker away just like CPS did. Like Robert did. I couldn't lose him again."

She wrung her hands together as her eyes met her son's, and the tears fell faster than ever. "I… I can't lose him. When you told me I couldn't work for you anymore, it felt like my heart was literally breaking. There was pain in my chest, I swear. I don't think I could take it if I couldn't be with him."

Walker whimpered.

"Mama loves you," she said to the baby, but didn't reach for him.

He felt like a monster. "Here. Take him." Brax handed Walker over rather than torture Tessa any longer.

"Thank you, thank you." She closed her eyes, kissing the baby's cheeks and forehead.

Anyone with eyes could see she adored her son. Brax's heart softened. If he had been in her position, what would he have done? How many people would he have lied to if he felt powerless to do anything else?

She opened her eyes. "The people looking for Robert are the ones who took my purse at the mall. They were using my phone to track me. They don't know about you and Robert being brothers, and they don't know the baby is here. I made sure of that."

That was enough for him. She could've told those

thugs about him to get them to leave her alone. Instead, she'd chosen to protect him.

He folded his arms. "No more secrets."

She shook her head. "No more secrets."

"Okay." When he draped an arm over her shoulders and led her to the house, she didn't shrug away from his touch. "We'll work this out together."

Chapter Fifteen

Telling the truth hadn't been easy. Putting it out there and hoping Brax would understand. Leaving her life in his hands.

Tessa kissed Walker for the fiftieth time since Brax had handed him to her. Coming clean had been worth the fear. And this was her reward.

"Come on, buddy," she whispered, guiding the bottle to Walker's mouth. "Let's have our dinner so you can go to bed."

Brax was on the phone, pacing the kitchen. She could hear him down there from the nursery, though there was no making out exactly what he said.

It was enough to know he believed her. And she'd believed him when he'd told her so. This wasn't a game to lure her into trusting him.

"There I was," she whispered to Walker with a smile, "thinking he'd call the cops before I even finished, you know? I just knew he wouldn't believe me. That he would take you away. But he surprised me."

Brax's deep voice reverberated from downstairs.

"He's a surprising man," she concluded as Walker finished his bottle.

She burped and changed him before putting him down to sleep. His fine hair was so soft under her fingers as she stroked his head. "I love you so much. Nobody's going to take you away again. You know how I know? Because your uncle Brax is on it now."

He was in the process of wrapping things up on the phone when she went downstairs. "We'll touch base on that first thing in the morning. For now, let's look up the paperwork involved in the custody case and follow up with CPS about the reports."

He turned to her when she reached the doorway leading from the dining room. "They're on it. And once my brothers decide to get to the bottom of something, consider it done."

"I can't thank you enough. For everything."

He cocked an eyebrow, eyes twinkling. "What did I do?"

"Are you kidding? Or is this your way of getting me to list everything you've done for me so far?" She held up a hand, counting off on her fingers. "You gave me somewhere to live when I had literally nowhere to go. You believed me when you could've easily called the cops and turned your back on me. You called your brothers and got them on the case. And this won't be the end of it. You'll find ways to keep amazing me."

It was gratifying, the way his charming smile slid into sheepishness. "Don't worry about it. I know Robert, and I'm so very sorry he hurt you."

There was no way to answer that, so she shrugged it off. "I'm starving. I can get something together for us."

"Don't bother with that." He placed his hands on her shoulders and steered her to the table. "Take a seat. I'll handle dinner."

"You don't have to do that."

"You deserve to have somebody take care of you after everything you've been through. It's the least I can do." He bent, looking through the fridge. "Though I can't guarantee it'll be gourmet cuisine. We're a little low on supplies. I didn't plan on coming back until tomorrow."

"I don't need anything gourmet." She rested her head on her palm, watching him. There was something to be said for a man who knew his way around the kitchen.

Especially when the man in question looked like Brax.

He eyed her while opening a jar of spaghetti sauce. "You had a little time to talk with Mom today. Did she scare you off?"

Tessa laughed softly, since the opposite was true. "I doubt she could scare anybody off."

"Think again. But you're not a teenager with an attitude, so it's probably different for you."

"I guess she had to be pretty tough to keep you guys in line."

"We didn't always make it easy on her." He poured the sauce into a pan and covered it, setting it aside while a larger pot filled with water in the sink. "But somehow, she and Dad made it work. And let me tell you, I never imagined I'd look at my brothers as anything but strangers. Now? They're more my brothers than Robert will ever be."

She frowned at the sound of his name. It was sort of a habit. "How the two of you could share DNA is beyond me."

"I think being half brothers helps—and the fact that we weren't raised together. We didn't even know about each other until I did one of those genetic test things a few years back."

"Oh, really?"

"Yeah, one of those late-night impulse decisions. Ordering the test, spitting into a tube." He lifted a shoulder like it didn't matter, but Tessa noticed the way he averted his eyes. It had obviously mattered, finding his blood relatives.

"So you share a…"

"Father. He was an affair my mom had. Or rather, my father was already married to Robert's mother."

She winced. "I see."

"He never acknowledged me. I was nine when my mother died. Without a father willing to claim me and no other family, I went into foster care."

"I'm really sorry."

Another shrug. He salted the pasta water before turning to the pantry. "I had a hard time. I thought I was a pretty tough kid by the time Mom and Dad took me in. The Pattersons, I mean. Two years on the streets and in some sketchy foster homes had hardened me, and life hadn't exactly been easy before then."

"But you came around."

"I did. It wasn't easy for anybody, of course, but I got there. I was one of the lucky ones."

He turned to her with a sigh, concern etched on his handsome face. Even more handsome now that he knew about her past and hadn't turned her away.

Before now, she couldn't have imagined him being more attractive than he already was, since he'd been heart-stopping the second she'd laid eyes on him.

"To be honest, that's one of the reasons we all want to help Walker. He told me you were dead. It never occurred to me to fact check that info. And if I refused to take custody or accused Robert of dropping him on me and lying about our arrangement, Walker would've gone into foster care. Nobody wanted that."

She shivered at the thought. "Thank you again, then. For taking care of my son."

"Hey, he's a cute kid. And just about as smart as his uncle, but not quite."

"Considering he's barely more than five months old, I don't know what that says about you."

It was good to hear Brax laugh, and it felt good to laugh along with him. If it wasn't for the whole Robert-on-the-run situation, they might be any other couple in the world enjoying a quiet night together.

Wow. Had she just thought of them as a couple?

"Like I said, nothing fancy." Brax brought a steaming bowl of spaghetti to the table to go with the salad he'd already prepared and freshly warmed rolls.

"Nothing fancy? I lived on cereal and instant noodles for way longer than I feel comfortable admitting. This is a feast."

Tessa attacked her food. It wasn't until then that she realized that she hadn't had much of an appetite for a long time. The weight of secrets and fear had been heavy.

"I have to ask you something." He rested his elbows on the table, and she didn't think it would be right to correct him. "What attracted you to Robert? I know you said he was charming."

Yes, he used to be, and now that Tessa understood the specifics of his relationship to Brax, she knew their father must've been a real handsome devil of a man. He'd passed those looks on to both of his sons, along with his charm.

"What else did I need?" She shrugged. "Like I said, I was lonely. He must've seen that in me. Some people know how to home in on that and take advantage."

"He's the type, of that I have no doubt." Brax shook his head in disgust as he took his plate to the sink.

Funny how his father had passed on his selfishness to Robert but not to Brax.

Brax was good. Honest. Decent. Even after being hit with some of the worst life had to offer, he hadn't become hard and cold.

"At least let me help with the dishes," she offered,

bringing her plate to the sink. "How about you dry? I'll wash up."

"You won't get an argument out of me." He grinned. "I hate washing dishes. I'll cook all day, but I'd have to use disposable plates."

She only shook her head with a smile. "Let me guess, washing dishes was one of your chores as a kid."

"How'd you know?" he asked as she giggled helplessly.

"Cooking was my chore once I was old enough to handle it. But unlike you, that only made me love it."

"That's because it's possible to lend a little imagination to cooking, and it's a lot more gratifying. There's only so many ways to wash a dish. It's not much fun."

"It can be." She shrugged, biting back a smile.

"How?"

She splashed him with sudsy water. "That's how!"

"No fair!" He reached into the sink and splashed her, then blew a mountain of suds toward her face.

Laughing uncontrollably, she tried to duck out of the way, but the wet floor had ideas of its own. She slipped, arms pinwheeling as she lost control of her body.

"Careful!" Brax was still laughing when he caught her before she hit the floor. "See? That's what you get for trying to be cute."

She looked up into his shining eyes, breathless and giggling and having more fun than she'd had in a very long time. Something she saw there silenced her. She could hardly breathe.

He hooked a finger under her chin, tipping her head back. Her eyes drifted to his lips a heartbeat before those lips touched hers.

He was so different from Robert.

The fact that Robert came into her thoughts at all seemed like a sacrilege, but there was no helping the comparison at first. It came up on its own, without her consciously thinking about it.

Robert had been slick. Forcing his way into her mouth like he was staking a claim on her. Caring only about how it made him feel. Brax was in an entirely different league—no big surprise, since he was in a different league in every other way imaginable.

He took his time, moving his lips against hers in a firm but gentle way. Wanting, but not forcing. Coaxing her.

The hand under her chin cupped her cheek while the other pressed against the small of her back and pulled her closer. She reveled in it, since there was no way to be close enough to him. Her hands rested against his chest where his heart hammered away. Hers did too, slamming against her ribs, leaving her weak and fluttery.

It was the most thrilling sensation. The sort of first kiss a woman dreamed about after reading about it in books or seeing it in movies. The sort of kiss she'd never imagined anybody would give her.

When his arm tightened around her and the kiss deepened, her entire body came alive. Yes, this was what she wanted. This was right and perfect. The scent of his cologne, his warm breath on her face, the sense of safety in his strong arms.

It ended too soon.

She leaned in a little further, chasing after what he was taking away. Her heart ached almost as much as her unsatisfied body.

"I'm sorry," Brax murmured, stroking her cheek one more time before letting his hands fall to his sides.

"Is it me?" she whispered. Was she not what he wanted?

"Oh, no. No, that's not it at all." He crammed his fists into his pockets, shoulders raised near his ears. "Believe me. I want you, Tessa. Badly."

"You do?"

He managed a faint smile. "Too much, maybe. But it wouldn't be right this way. You're caught up in a situation beyond your control. Let's get that settled and clear your name, and then we can focus on…us. If that's what you want."

That was what she wanted—that and so much more.

Before she could say anything to embarrass herself, the sound of Walker's cries came from the monitor on the counter. It was almost a relief having an excuse to leave the kitchen and gather herself a little. She made a quick escape with her cheeks still flushed and her lips tingling from Brax's kiss.

Just when she thought there couldn't be more of a reason to clear her name.

Chapter Sixteen

Two days of looking into Tessa's story had left Brax more certain of one thing than he'd ever been: Robert needed a good throttling. He'd needed one for a long time.

"I knew he wasn't exactly a sweetheart," he murmured, passing files back and forth among his brothers. "But this takes being a rotten human being to a new level."

"He's playing in the pros," Luke grunted.

"He could manage an entire team." Chance blew out a low whistle at the report of the accident that had killed Tessa's parents. "Wild. No matter how many times I see something like this, it always shakes me up a little. One minute they were on their way to dinner. The next? It's over."

Brax only half heard his brother's musings. What concerned him was Tessa. How it must've felt to lose her parents so suddenly. How terrified she must've been. How alone.

One of those little reminders of life's unpredictability. "Never get too comfortable. You never know when it'll end."

"Wow." Weston rubbed his temples with a rueful grin. "We're a cheerful team today."

Brax sank into the chair behind his desk. "What I can't understand is why Robert would go to all the trouble of taking Walker away—setting Tessa up, concocting stories for CPS—if he was planning on leaving the kid with me. He stole his son. Not an easy thing to do, and punishable by law if it turns out the reports were faked. Up to two years in jail, a sizable fine. He took a real risk."

"He probably didn't count on getting himself in trouble." Luke shrugged. "Though knowing him, even as little as I do, I can't imagine why, considering he was always in trouble for something or other."

"Arrogant." Weston sighed. "That sort of person has to be arrogant. They have to believe they're untouchable. That they'll be able to get out of any situation—and, of course, that this close call will be the last close call. Their luck will turn around."

"A lot of good that's ever done him," Luke muttered, flipping through the falsified reports Robert had called in. "He'd gone into detail too, like it had taken real thought to put this plan together."

When Brax looked over the signature on the paperwork terminating Tessa's parental rights, that part made a lot more sense. "Look who it is. Robert's cousin Ray. He must've coached Robert on what to say, how to make an effective case."

"At least that works in Tessa's favor," Weston

pointed out. "It'll take time, no doubt, but just the fact that the judge is Robert's cousin is a positive for us. No way should anyone remotely related to one of the parties be involved in a legal proceeding."

"I know that'll make her happy." She deserved a little happiness, a little hope, after everything Robert had put her through.

He looked around at his brothers. "So, the best we can come up with is Robert didn't figure on getting himself in trouble and having to leave town. I guess running with a baby would slow him down."

Luke nodded. "I guess we can assume it wasn't for Walker's sake that he ended up on your doorstep."

"Let's say that if Robert took his son's safety into consideration, I'd just about fall over in surprise." Brax smiled, but it was a grim smile. Bitter.

There were people out in the world just dying to have kids of their own, while others treated their children like possessions. Pawns to be used in a larger game.

Just as there were men like his biological father who refused to accept a son's existence and left him to suffer out of sheer selfishness.

"I can't believe Tessa kept all this to herself." Luke shook his head. "So much for one person to carry on their shoulders."

Brax nodded. "She's been through a lot. I wonder what those thugs must've thought when she didn't scare easily. And the way she slipped past them and out of Eagle Pass."

Even he could hear the pride in his voice. He *was* proud of her. She'd done well.

Once he was alone in his office, he opened his laptop and pulled up the list of dates Tessa had been terrorized. He'd asked her to compile the list in case there was a way of cross-referencing those dates with security footage in the areas in which she'd been accosted or attacked.

License plates, images of the men involved, anything—as long as he could get an idea of exactly who they were dealing with. It had been too dark to make out much about the two attackers who'd found Tessa in his car.

Brax wanted to see them. To know them before he taught them what happened to men who terrorized women.

He recognized one of the dates immediately. The night they'd gone to Nick's. Her account of the situation confirmed this. She'd been inside the office building with Walker when two men had tried to get inside.

He sat up straighter, eager now, digging into the network to find their security footage. There were cameras mounted at each corner of the building, along with one over the front door. Perfect.

"There you are," he muttered, staring at the men. One who glared in through the window, one who tried to force the door open.

The longer he studied them, going back and forth through the feed from all three cameras, the more certain he was that these were the men who'd attacked him behind the strip mall.

One of them had a pockmarked face—Tessa had mentioned him, had described what he'd done to her outside the mall before taking her purse. He was the one who'd tried to open the doors.

Brax was no expert in body language or reading facial expressions, but he knew pure frustration when he saw it. The sort of frustration that could turn into violence with little provocation.

Knowing she'd been inside the building and able to see the men who wanted to hurt her sent his blood pressure soaring. Oh, yeah, he was going to enjoy teaching them what happened to men who terrorized women.

He rolled back the footage in hopes of catching sight of the car the men had arrived in, but it was out of the camera's range.

He switched to another camera, this one mounted at the corner of the building, and rolled the footage back to before he'd arrived with Walker. Just in case the car had passed in the distance, in case they'd been watching even then.

It wasn't the two men he ended up catching sight of. It was Tessa, emerging from the alley next to the office building. Where had she come from?

He switched feeds, watching her emerge from the alley from a different angle. But there was no footage of her entering the alley, like she would if she'd come up behind the building.

He moved to the camera at the other end of the

alley, mounted at the rear of the building, and watched the timestamp at the top of the screen. She hadn't entered the alley from back there.

So where had she come from?

A sick feeling bloomed in the pit of Brax's stomach. He rolled the footage back to the time they'd left the office together earlier that night.

There they were, talking. He'd asked if she could come in early, and she had accepted. Then he'd walked away, carrying Walker to the car. Tessa had watched for a moment or two before turning and heading for the alley. Only she'd never come out at the other end.

No wonder it had been so easy for her to get to the office in a hurry. And why she hadn't even let him finish asking her to move in before accepting. It wasn't just motherly love.

She'd been sleeping in the alley all along.

His fists tightened hard enough to make his joints ache. Robert had so much to pay for.

Brax was still furious enough when his phone rang that he practically barked into it on answering. "Yeah?"

"Brax. It's Janice Morgan."

He forced his anger away. "Hi. How's it going?"

"About as well as can be expected when dealing with the Riviera cartel." She sighed. Somehow, the DA sounded even more exhausted than she had the last time they'd spoken—considering that he'd noted her exhaustion then, too, that was saying something.

"What happened?"

"Our shopkeeper passed away last night."

He closed his eyes, stricken. "I'm sorry to hear that."

"So am I, considering that the poor guy was recovering well as of yesterday afternoon. I checked in with his doctors to see about his progress, and they were pleased with the way things were going. They told me he might be able to go home as early as tomorrow."

"You're kidding."

"It happens that way sometimes," she allowed. "But the doctors expressed surprise when I talked to them a few minutes ago."

"We know what we're talking about, then."

"I think we can safely say this has 'the cartel' written all over it."

He couldn't think of anything to say except to offer a single reassurance. "You can count on me. I don't plan on backing down from testifying."

"Thank you for that—but remember, be careful. Now's the time to grow an extra pair of eyes in the back of your head. With Prince out on bail until the trial, there's no telling what else he's put into motion."

He took this to heart and was still thinking about it hours later when he left for the night. A quick call home confirmed everything was okay there. Tessa and Walker were waiting.

They were quickly becoming the center of his world, if they hadn't already firmly planted themselves there. What a time to need eyes in the back of his head.

The ride home normally helped clear his mind. It wasn't a heavily traveled route—he liked it that way, liked not having to sit in traffic the way some commuters did.

The wash of high beams took him by surprise, almost blinding him when the light hit the rearview mirror. He threw an arm up, blinking hard to clear away the spots in his vision.

"What do you think you're doing?" he asked, tapping the horn. Some people...

His car jolted forward, pushed by the car behind him.

That was no accident.

He floored the gas, determined to outrun them. There was an on-ramp for the freeway about a mile ahead. He could lose the tail there.

The driver had other ideas, ramming him harder than before and almost driving Brax off the road. He corrected in time, swinging the wheel to the left, kicking up clouds of dust. In the end, though, it gave the car behind him just enough room to slide in alongside and force him into the ditch.

Brax's chest hit the wheel when the car pitched forward, and pain exploded in his shoulder when he hit the door. He pushed the pain aside and brought the car to a stop.

His heart hammered wildly. At least the adrenaline kept the pain at bay, but he knew that he'd be bruised come morning. If he made it to morning.

Looking around, he tried to spot the car that had caused this. There was light up on the road, telling him they'd come to a stop with the high beams still on. The best thing to do was stay in the car, doors locked. He was armed, but there was no way of telling how many people were up there.

Was this because of Robert? Or Prince Riviera?

He found out soon enough. A familiar figure reached the edge of the road, standing just where it dropped off into the ditch. The high beams created a sort of halo around him. But there was nothing holy about the head of the Riviera cartel.

Prince stared down at Brax's car. What was he waiting for? To see how badly Brax was hurt?

How had the cartel found him?

Rather than descending to the car or sending somebody down in his place, Prince called out from where he stood, "You have the choice not to testify."

With that, he walked away, and seconds later the sound of a car door closing came as a relief. The glow of the headlights faded to darkness, leaving Brax alone.

Chapter Seventeen

It was so quiet at night. Blessedly quiet. Better than
an alley. Or the back seat of a car.

Tessa propped her head up on one bent arm, staring up at the ceiling. How much time had passed
since she'd gone to bed? Hours, probably.

Hours of worrying. Wondering.

What was Brax hiding from her?

Something was going on. He had that tense, cagey
energy about him, the way he'd acted while tracking
that bail jumper. Like something was very wrong.
Whatever it was, he wasn't sharing it with her.

And that left her feeling slightly insulted. Wasn't
he the one who'd made her promise there would be
no more secrets? Yet there he was a few days later
acting secretive, putting up an invisible wall between
them.

Why?

Naturally, her mind went first to the most likely
answer: he blamed her for what had happened with
Robert. Given time to think things over, he'd decided she was untrustworthy and too stupid or gull-
ible to care about.

Why else would he have been so distracted when he'd gotten home from work last night? Distant. Like he was only half with her, half someplace else.

Weston had called to tell her Brax had had car trouble and would be late getting home. While she'd appreciated the call, why couldn't Brax call for himself? Was he that dismissive of her?

He'd acted like it after finally showing up. She might as well have not been there at all. So much for looking forward to him getting home.

Not that he'd been mean or rude. That might've been easier to deal with. She was used to rude men. Being ignored, especially by Brax, wasn't as easy to swallow.

He'd gone to bed not long after getting home. He hadn't eaten, but that didn't seem to matter half as much as getting away from her had. His movements had been stiff, like there was something physically wrong.

He hadn't told her what it was. He'd hardly said a word.

She'd hoped to ask him about it in the morning, but he'd been gone by the time she'd woken up. That was early even for him.

He'd worked late again, not getting home until nearly ten o'clock. So yeah, seemed like he was avoiding her. If he hadn't been so different before then—friendly, warm, curious about her and about how her day had gone—this sudden change wouldn't have come as such a shock.

It looked like the more time he had to think about what she'd told him, the more distant he'd become.

Even now, lying in a darkened bedroom, just the thought of Brax losing respect for her and thinking she couldn't be trusted was enough to make her chest ache. Tears stung behind her eyes. All they did was frustrate her.

Her stomach started growling. She hadn't eaten dinner. She'd waited for Brax until it was clear he wouldn't be home, and then decided to sleep instead. The stew was in the fridge now, though that wasn't exactly what she wanted to eat at this time of night.

Or the morning. She'd finally checked the time—usually, she avoided looking at the clock since it only made her more anxious while she was lying awake—and found she'd been staring at the ceiling for three hours. It was almost half past two.

The thought of Walker waking up before the sun wasn't pleasant, but now that her stomach was growling, she knew sleep wouldn't be coming. Only eating would settle her down. She tiptoed downstairs in the dark house toward the faint glow of the kitchen. She was careful to be quiet, not wanting to take a chance on waking up Walker or Brax.

She stopped short when she saw Brax in the kitchen, bent over in front of the fridge like he'd had the same idea about food. He hadn't eaten dinner either.

The impulse to run swept over her. Why did her mind go there right away? Why would she run from him? He was the last person she should want to avoid.

Two days ago, she would've laughed at the idea. But that was before he'd started ignoring her.

He didn't know she was there. She could get away and sneak back upstairs and avoid any awkwardness. She would have if it hadn't been for something rooting her to the floor.

Him wearing low-slung sweatpants that looked like they were a moment away from sliding off his hips. No shirt. She could make out the lines of his slim waist, broad shoulders and muscular arms in the light from the refrigerator.

She could hardly breathe. Her mouth went dry. Good thing, since she might've started drooling otherwise.

He looked back at her over his shoulder. "Oh. Hi."

She struggled to respond. "Hi," she murmured.

Brax turned toward her and the sight of his left side made her gasp. A mass of bruises covered his shoulder and arm, then bloomed again on his chest and ribs. There were lacerations along his biceps and elbow. It was ugly and had to be painful.

"What happened to you?" she whispered with her heart in her throat. Seeing him that way was enough to cause her actual pain. If she had only known…

He looked down at himself, wincing. "Yeah." He frowned, cleared his throat, looked anywhere but at her. "That car trouble I had two nights ago?"

"Yeah?"

"It was more like an accident."

"Brax!"

"I'm fine."

"Fine?" She gestured to him. "You don't look fine. No wonder you walked around like a reanimated corpse when you got home. How did it happen? What sort of accident?"

"It was nothing." He still wasn't looking at her. "One of those things. Dark, empty road. Driving too fast. I get a little cocky sometimes, I guess."

She studied him. Watched his subtle movements.

He was lying.

"There aren't many things I'm really good at," she admitted in a low voice. "But if there's anything I know, it's when somebody's lying. You'd think I would've been smarter about Robert because of that, but…" She shrugged, then pointed at him. "You're not telling the truth. Come on. You got away from those thugs who were following us without coming close to another car. You're an excellent driver."

He shrugged. "Things happen."

"You won't look at me. That's another way I can tell you're hiding something. No secrets. That was your rule. I can follow it. Can you?"

"You're tough." He sighed before finally looking her in the eye. "Okay. I wanted to keep you out of it, but I see that's a waste of time. I didn't run off the road. I was run off the road. By Prince Riviera."

Her heart sank like a stone. "Oh, no. Brax…"

"I'm okay. See?" He spread his arms—even now, in the back of her mind, she couldn't help but notice how very okay he looked.

Except for the hideous bruises that monster had given him.

"Why don't you sit down?" She reached out and took one of his hands. "Come on. I'll make you a sandwich. You need to eat, no matter how stressed you are."

"I'd argue, but I really am hungry. You should be asleep, though."

She giggled softly while pulling food from the fridge. "Why do you think I came down in the first place?"

He was quiet for a while as she put turkey and Swiss cheese together. "I'm sorry," he eventually mumbled as she put the finishing touches on the sandwich and cut it in half.

"For what?"

"For keeping you in the dark. I didn't know what to do or how to manage this, so I figured it was better to keep you out of it."

"I understand." Her relief was almost physical. Not relief at him being hurt, but at there being a reason he had avoided her. Especially since that reason was to protect her.

She started with her own sandwich, but a glance in his direction stopped her. "You okay?" she asked when he winced as he rubbed his neck.

"Stiff, you know? Nothing I can't manage."

"So stoic." She went to him. "Eat your sandwich. I'll rub your neck."

"As long as you can manage not to strangle me."

"Don't tempt me."

She was already massaging his neck before the realization that she was touching him registered on her awareness. It was innocent, of course, but still. He was shirtless and she was very close to him, and her heart didn't know what to do with that.

"This is a great sandwich," he grunted around a mouthful of food. "Just what I needed."

"I'm glad."

He looked up at her, touching one hand to hers. "I needed this too."

"I'm not very good at it."

"You're just fine." He pulled her around and into his lap before she could think to stop him.

Not that she would've wanted to stop him. Not for anything.

Even so, she had to know. "You told me a few nights ago you didn't want us to go anywhere until all these problems were worked out."

"I did say that." His arms locked around her, pulling her close to his bare chest.

She touched a gentle hand to his bruised shoulder. "This doesn't look like things are worked out."

"Sometimes I wish I'd keep my mouth shut," he grumbled.

There was no way to fight it. Not that she tried very hard or wanted to try.

Not when she was so close to him, and he was so warm and firm and strong.

His face filled her awareness an instant before his lips met hers and pulled her down, down into a sweet, soft kiss. Maybe it was two days spent thinking he hated her that made it so sweet. So special.

Soreness didn't seem to slow him down. His arms

tightened as the kiss deepened. She was careful not to hurt him but couldn't possibly resist the urge to touch him. To feel for herself his smooth skin, the muscles warm underneath.

She was hungry for more than a sandwich. The sort of hunger he stirred in her couldn't be satisfied by anything but him.

Her hunger deepened. The way he kissed her. The way he held her. The way his hand burned a trail down her back. Would she ever be able to get enough of him? Or would every touch and kiss leave her wanting more? The way they did now.

There was nothing in the world that could've stopped them.

Except for somebody who couldn't speak, but could certainly make his presence known.

Tessa giggled when Walker's cries came through the monitor. "He has a sixth sense, I swear."

Brax blew out a sigh, then laughed. "His timing is impeccable."

"He's probably hungry. It's almost three. I could heat up a bottle."

There wasn't much she felt less like doing than working her way off Brax's lap, but it had to be done. What was she going to do otherwise? Their first time couldn't be on the kitchen floor.

By the time she had water simmering on the stove and the bottle warming up in the pan, Brax brought Walker down to the kitchen.

She tried not to care that Brax now wore a T-shirt, but it wasn't easy.

"Hey, buddy. You hungry?" Tessa stroked Walker's smooth, soft cheek before kissing the top of his head.

"Yeah, he was telling me upstairs he had a craving for a turkey sandwich, but I reminded him about the whole teeth thing. They help when it comes to chewing." The way Brax smiled at the baby melted her heart.

The three of them jumped when one of the living room windows shattered.

Brax handed a screaming Walker to her and positioned himself between her and the living room. Tessa might've screamed a little, too, out of surprise, but it was all a blur.

She followed a step behind Brax as they moved toward the sound. Her heart raced, and her stomach churned as she clutched Walker to her chest, cupping his tiny head and tucking it under her chin.

His arm shot out, stopping her before they reached the living room.

The smell of gasoline and burning carpet filled her nose. A dancing, flickering light reflected off the walls.

Fire.

Chapter Eighteen

Fire was spreading in the living room, catching the throw rug, the curtains. Brax caught sight of a terrified Tessa holding a screaming Walker.

The smell of gasoline almost overwhelmed them. It must have been a Molotov cocktail that had smashed through the window. Common sense told him to get out of the house, but his gut told him somebody was outside. Waiting. Planning to do more harm than the fire.

Acting purely on instinct, he steered Tessa and the baby back into the kitchen. "Stay in here." He shoved them into the pantry. It was safer in there: no windows, no way for anybody to get to them from outside.

But also no way to escape if the fire raged out of control.

"The fire!" Tessa clung to Walker as he squalled.

"I'll handle it. Stay in here." He closed the door and ran into the living room. Grabbing a pillow off the couch, he flailed at the fire on the rug and the bits of curtain that had fallen to the floor.

The room was smoky, but the fire hadn't spread. Whoever had thrown the bottle hadn't tossed it hard enough for the glass to shatter when it hit the floor.

Lucky break. Literally.

Once he was sure the fire was out, he moved to his safe, took out his gun and slid his back along the wall to a window. The soft light from the kitchen glowed behind him as he peered out into the moonless night.

"Where are you?" he muttered to himself. No one would go to the trouble of sending a message like this without sticking around to see if the message had been received.

Through one of the front windows, he caught the outline of a car sitting on the road leading away from the house. Far enough away that they'd be safe from the fire, but not so far that they couldn't pick him off if he'd bolted from his burning home.

Hugging the wall again, he made his way back to the kitchen for the one phone he knew he could always find: his landline. He punched the speed dial button for Chance.

"Can't talk long," he barked. "Somebody threw a Molotov cocktail through my living room window. It's not terrible, but I need you to call the fire department and the cops and get them out here. You guys too. I think whoever did this is hanging out waiting for me."

Chance let out a string of curses before asking, "What's your next move?"

"I have to get Tessa and Walker out of here." He

coughed on thickening smoke. He must have missed a smoldering ember. "Make the call. I have to get out."

"Be careful."

Brax returned to the living room. The curtains had reignited and the wall behind them had started to blacken. He fought through the building fear and focused on the only thing—the only people—who mattered right now: Tessa and Walker.

Why was Walker so quiet? Had someone gotten to them?

Forgetting about the flames that threatened to burn his home to the ground, Brax raced to the kitchen and flung open the pantry door. Tessa, sitting cross-legged on the floor, fed Walker the bottle she'd been warming before the chaos had erupted. Even in the middle of a blazing hellscape, her first concern had been for her son.

And somebody wanted to hurt them. His rage alone could've set the house on fire all by itself.

"Come on. We have to get out of here," he whispered through clenched teeth, careful not to scare the baby again.

"What are we going to do?" Tessa's eyes widened with terror.

That was a good question. "We'll go out the back. There's someone waiting in a car in the front."

He reached down to help her up and hurried toward the kitchen door. Before rushing outside, he paused to check the backyard. It was clear. So far. "Keep him as quiet as you can and follow me. Don't say a word."

Even though everything looked quiet behind the house, he constantly scanned the area and listened hard, but he didn't pick up the slightest hint of an intruder. Riviera's men were either lazy or stupid.

No surprise. Not that Brax was in any position to complain.

He took Tessa's arm and led her away from the house as he continued to survey the grounds. Every crunch, every footstep rang out like a gong.

Somebody would be sent to cover the back when nobody had come running out of the front—Brax was sure of it, so he wasn't surprised when he heard a heavy tread coming their way from the side of the house. Brax pushed Tessa toward the trees. "Go!" he whispered. She darted off.

He turned and crouched behind a massive smoker that had provided the food for so many raucous gatherings, praying that Walker didn't choose this moment to become raucous himself.

Nobody was going to hurt his family.

He waited, hardly daring to breathe, gun at the ready. A tall, heavyset man rounded the corner with a cigarette hanging out of his mouth like he was taking a walk in the park. A Sunday stroll.

Brax used this to his advantage, waiting for the man to pass him before hitting him across the back of the head with the butt of his gun. The man crumpled at Brax's feet.

There was no one with him. No one following close behind. Everybody was out front waiting in that car.

For a split second, Brax was torn. Part of him wanted to make this goon—and all of the goons waiting in the car—pay for threatening his family, but the bigger part urged him to run for the trees so he could be with Tessa and the baby. They were too vulnerable out there, even while hiding.

The goons or Tessa and Walker?

Tessa and Walker of course. "Tessa?" he whispered once he was close enough to risk speaking.

"Over here." He could just make out the sound of her voice. "He's sleeping."

Tessa crouched between a pair of thick tree trunks, so hidden in the deep shadows he almost tripped over her before realizing she was there.

He squatted next to her and wrapped his arms around them both. "You okay?"

"Fine." The trembling he felt under his hands told a different story. She was still terrified.

Smoke billowed from the house now, drifting out through the broken window. Another window shattered as the flames grew. He hated thinking of what was happening to his home, but what truly mattered was with him in his arms.

They were his, both of them, and he would die if it meant keeping them safe.

He stiffened at the sight of the unconscious man stirring, working his way to his knees. "Shh," he hissed into Tessa's ear. A glance at Walker showed he was fast asleep now that he'd eaten.

A second man came around from the other side

of the house. "Hey, what are you doing?" His voice carried toward them as he helped his buddy up.

"…hit me…don't know where he went…" The guy sounded confused, dazed. He was lucky. Brax would've liked to have done a lot worse to him—to both of those thugs.

"It's okay," he whispered to Tessa, his arms tightening around her and the baby. "We're safe. They can't hurt us."

She nodded then buried her face into his neck. It was better that way. For her to hide her eyes and pretend none of this was happening. Otherwise, the baby might sense her agitation, and there was no telling how long their safety would last once he started screaming.

Sirens wailing in the distance calmed most of Brax's anxiety. Beyond the house, he could make out the faint glow of the red lights on top of the fire trucks. The men froze for a second before taking off. It was the first smart thing they'd done all night.

When they were out of sight, Brax breathed a little easier, but there was no way he was going to lead Tessa and Walker out into the open before he knew with absolute certainty that they were safe. Which meant waiting and watching and listening.

It wasn't until Weston and Luke appeared that he stood, helping Tessa to her feet. "We're here!" he called out to them.

Seeing his brothers chased away the last of his apprehension. It also brought the grim realization that he could have lost Tessa and Walker. Now that he could think straight, now that their safety was assured, he could afford to think about what might have happened.

What if they'd all been upstairs asleep when the Molotov cocktail had come through the window? What if Tessa had been in the kitchen alone with Walker, fixing his bottle? Would she have panicked and run out the front door?

So many what-ifs bombarded him, it was a relief to be distracted by the pair of officers looking for answers.

He told them everything he could. He described both men he'd seen behind the house and what little he had been able to make out of the car that had been parked on the dirt road.

"What reason would anyone have to attack you and your family, Mr. Patterson?" one officer asked.

His family. That was what they were. He didn't bother correcting the officer who'd asked.

"I'm scheduled to be the prime witness against Prince Riviera and his cartel," he explained. "District Attorney Morgan will tell you all about it if you give her a call. Riviera and his men ran me off the road two nights ago." He pulled up his shirt to show them his chest.

"Why didn't you alert us to that before now? This could've been prevented," the second officer said.

Weston spoke before Brax could, and that was for the best. "We've worked most of the past thirty-six hours straight trying to figure out how to protect my brother without making the situation worse for him or the people close to him."

When he looked at Tessa and Walker, the officer softened. But not by much. "All the more reason to bring us in on this."

"The shopkeeper who was set to testify went to you—" Brax cut himself off when Weston shot him a look.

No. He wasn't helping things by mouthing off.

Though he believed he had a strong point.

"We'll pick up Riviera now that we have a statement based on the encounter you had with him," the second officer stated. "We can offer protection."

"I've already arranged for a safe house," Weston assured them. "That's the first step. You take care of Riviera and his men. We'll take care of our own."

Chance wrapped Tessa and Walker with a blanket he'd brought from his car.

Luke looked grim when he approached Brax. "It could've been much worse."

"I know."

"It's going to take some work to restore the living room. You did well putting out what you could before getting out."

"I couldn't let the place burn down with Tessa and Walker in it." Just the thought made Brax's stomach twist.

Luke clapped a hand over Brax's uninjured shoulder. "I know what you're going through, brother. I know how it is to feel like there's somebody whose safety is more important than your own. Not that it helps you any, but... I understand."

It didn't help. Not in any concrete way. But it did ease Brax's mind a little. He wasn't completely out of his head for wanting to kill everybody involved in what had happened tonight. Not for his own sake. Not even for the sake of his home, which he'd always been proud of and thought of as a sanctuary.

But for them. For Tessa and Walker.

First and foremost, he had to get them to safety. Then he'd make it his mission in life to make sure something like this never happened again.

Chapter Nineteen

A police radio squawked. Tessa jumped at the sound. Her heart lodged in her throat. Her arms shook so hard she was afraid she might drop the baby.

She would break into a million pieces soon. All it would take would be one more thing. One more menacing face in the dark. One more emergency. One more panicked run at nighttime. It would destroy her.

Then there were the questions. The what-ifs. When she wasn't jumping at the slightest sound, she asked herself what could have happened.

If they hadn't been downstairs when the bomb had come through the window. If it had shattered on impact with the floor. If they'd gone out the wrong door and one of those men had cut them off. If Walker had cried out while they were hiding in the trees.

If, if, if. An endless string of them, stretching into infinity.

She'd lose her mind if this didn't stop. There was another what-if. What if this never stopped and she ended up losing what was left of her sanity?

No.

Some people had the luxury of falling apart when

life threw them curveballs. Some people didn't have a baby depending on them.

She nuzzled Walker's head, tucking it protectively under her chin, and marveled at his ability to sleep through so many things. A blessing, considering he'd fallen asleep while they'd been hiding. "Thank you, sweetheart," she whispered before kissing him.

Who had tried to kill them? Robert's enemies or Brax's? More than likely something so vicious would have come from the cartel, but there was no way to tell.

Did it matter? If they'd died, would it have mattered who had killed them? The result would've been the same.

A slight touch on her shoulder made her jump again.

"Sorry." Brax held up his hands, coming around in front of her. "I didn't mean to scare you."

A stunned little laugh bubbled up from her chest. "You're the least of my worries."

"Understood." His brows drew together. "Come on. Weston's going to get you two to a safe house. You'll be fine there."

Fine. As if anything could be fine. She almost laughed again, but the little bit of self-possession she still had told her it wouldn't be a good idea.

He walked her to Weston's car and opened the passenger side door for her to sit inside while Luke set up the car seat in the back. When Brax reached for Walker, she only held on tighter.

Brax's face fell, which was what got through to her. Knowing her reaction had hurt him. He had never done anything to hurt her or the baby. He didn't deserve this.

She extended her arms and held Walker out to him. Brax took the baby and fastened him into his car seat. He would be safe. Her son would be safe. Even if she still felt like she was going to fall apart.

The impulse to scurry over the center console, get behind the wheel, and tear off into the night with her son was so strong she almost couldn't resist it.

All that mattered was keeping him safe. She had to keep him safe. His life meant more than hers—after all, what had she ever done that was worth anything?

Giving birth to Walker had been the only worthwhile thing she'd ever done. He was her one good thing. And she'd come so close to losing him. Again.

She studied Brax's face as he looked down at her from outside the car. He had that look in his eyes. That sad, fallen sort of look like when she'd held Walker away from him. Brax hated this as much as she did. Maybe more, since he felt responsible. Nobody had to tell her that. She just knew.

He crouched beside the vehicle. "It's going to be okay, I swear. Once we get you and Walker to the safe house, there won't be anything to worry about."

His hand covered hers. "You're not in this alone. I'm going to keep you both safe. I swear on my life, Tessa. Nothing matters more to me than you and Walker. You're my priority, and I intend to make your safety my life's mission. Do you understand?"

The conviction in his words shook her to her core.

The strength in his voice. His confidence. A man with a mission was a powerful thing.

And he had the power to make her believe him.

She turned her hand upside down so they were palm-to-palm and laced her fingers with his. "Yes. I do."

"Good." He cupped her cheek with his free hand and sealed his promise with a kiss that soothed her aching heart.

"Let's roll." Weston slid behind the wheel. "Meet you there."

Brax gave his brother a nod, stood and looked at her one more time before closing the door. He lifted his hand in a wave before backing away.

"Don't worry. We'll split up on the way, just in case anybody's watching—which they aren't, but we can't be too careful." Weston stole a glance her way and cleared his throat. "Why don't you get some rest while we drive?"

"Where are we going? I mean, exactly where. Don't take it personally, I'm curious."

"I don't blame you. You have the right to be curious about where we're placing you for the time being. It's an apartment on the north side of San Antonio."

"Okay."

He eyed her. "Seriously. You look like you're ready to fall over."

"I didn't get any sleep tonight, even before this whole nightmare started."

"Then by all means." He gave her knee a gentle pat. "Rest while you can. Something tells me that come morning, your little guy isn't going to care very much what went on tonight."

He made a good point. Walker couldn't exactly tell time.

She'd close her eyes for just a minute…

"Tessa? We're here."

Her eyes snapped open. Not a second had passed. Or hadn't it? Because they were in a parking garage now. "Wow. I dropped right off."

"You needed it. Come on. Brax texted a few minutes ago. He's already inside." Weston helped with the car seat, and Tessa was all too happy to follow him into the apartment building.

"It's not the biggest or fanciest," Weston offered as he unlocked the door. Like he was apologizing in advance.

If she hadn't been half-dead from exhaustion, she might've told him this apartment was at least three times the size of the one she'd left in Eagle Pass. Furnished better too.

Brax was waiting, just like his brother had promised. He pulled her in for a hug. "You'll be safe here. I promise."

"I'm going to head out." Weston placed the car seat on the coffee table. "You have everything under control?"

"Sure." Brax shook his hand.

"Thank you," Tessa whispered. Weston touched two fingers to his temple in a quick salute before leaving them alone.

She turned to Brax with a heavy sigh. "Alone at last."

He offered a brief smile. "I hate to say it, but I'm going to have to leave you too."

"Really? Already?" Except a look over his shoulder told her it was close to dawn. It had been a long night.

"I'll be back soon. I promise."

She should let him go. She knew she should.

That didn't make it any easier to release the hold she had on his shirt.

"Tessa." He touched her hair, her face. "Nobody knows about this place except for people I trust—which pretty much means my brothers and that's it. You'll have to stay inside. No going out. But otherwise, you'll be safe here."

"I don't care that I can't leave. I'm worried about you."

His smile was more genuine now, and for a second he was his usual, charming self. "I'm the least of your worries, trust me. It's the bad guys you should be worried about."

"Unlikely." No amount of humor could ease the cold fist gripping her heart. "Please be careful."

"I will." He kissed her forehead and held her tight for a moment before letting her go. "I'm going to figure out how to keep us safe long-term. In the meantime, I'll send somebody with supplies for you and Walker. There's a burner phone on the nightstand in the bedroom that I'll call to contact you. All you have to do is sleep now. Okay?"

"Okay." She tried to be as brave as she could so he wouldn't have one more thing to worry about.

After all, she'd given him enough to worry about already.

IT WAS PAST noon when she woke up.

Her first thought, as always, was of Walker. He was next to her on the big bed, surrounded by pillows just in case he decided today was the day he'd start rolling all over the place.

"Hey, little man." She relaxed when she found him cooing to himself, playing with his feet. "I used to be that flexible once."

At least he was feeling good. No memory of last night's trauma.

That made one of them.

There was a message from Brax on the burner phone. Supplies on their way. Trusted sources.

Whatever that meant. She knew she could trust him—and anybody he trusted.

There was time to change Walker and take care of her own needs before a knock sounded at the front door. Tessa tiptoed to the door with her heart in her throat and peered out through the peephole.

It was Maci, from the office, along with a woman who looked vaguely familiar. They were loaded down with bags and boxes. She hurried to open the door so they could put everything down.

"Hi," Maci whispered as she hurried through to the kitchen. "Whew! That was my arm-day workout right there."

"You don't have to whisper. He's awake." Tessa went to the bedroom and brought Walker back.

"There he is! My best buddy!" Maci held out her arms, which didn't seem to be all that sore from carrying the packages after all.

Meanwhile, the other woman—small, blonde, with a face Tessa recognized from somewhere—held out a hand. "Hi. I'm Luke's fiancée, Claire Wallace."

Right. Tessa might've been half out of her mind with grief and pain after Robert had stolen Walker, but she remembered seeing Claire on the news around that time. There were stories about her supposedly killing somebody she'd worked with and then killing a cop, but she'd been cleared of all charges.

And had managed to simultaneously bring down one of the most crooked businessmen in Texas. Now Tessa understood how the woman had not only survived but had come out the other side smiling. She shook Claire's hand gladly.

"I've never seen Brax like this," Maci admitted as Claire and Tessa put the groceries and supplies away.

"Same here. I mean, I haven't known him for too long, but he's on a whole other level right now." Claire winced when she met Tessa's gaze. "Not to make you feel bad or anything. It isn't your fault."

"No, but he's definitely determined to get you out of this okay," Maci continued. "You have nothing to worry about. Believe me. Those boys do not give up."

Claire set aside the packs of diapers and wipes, then went back to stocking the pantry. "I'm surprised, honestly. Brax is usually the laid-back one, isn't he? I mean, I've always seen him that way. Charming and smiling. He could convince anybody of just about anything."

"True. Luke's usually the cranky one—with everybody but you, anyway," Maci teased with a wink at Claire. "Weston's Mr. Serious. And Chance…" She blew out a long sigh, rolling her eyes.

"You two don't get along well, do you?" Tessa asked, remembering them bickering during her time at the office.

"We get along fine. When I don't want to kill him."

Claire giggled. "Oh, please. You two have it bad for each other. You just don't want to admit it."

"'Oh, please' yourself!" Maci turned her attention to Walker, clearly eager to change the topic. Not fast enough, though, her flushed cheeks betraying her words.

Tessa exchanged a look with Claire. "I don't know," she said. "Sometimes it's those denied attractions that are the most explosive."

Claire's eyebrows moved up and down. "Remind me not to be around when a spark ignites the fuse."

"Okay, enough." Maci's face glowed redder as she turned back to them. "Believe me, I'm not the sort of woman a guy like Chance would ever look at twice. Men prefer women like you two, or didn't you know that?"

Tessa assumed Maci was referring to her figure, which could be described as plus-size. "You have curves I would kill for. Chance would be blind not to notice you."

"Anyway." Maci's voice was a little louder than it needed to be, which Tessa took as a signal that this part of the conversation was over. "Brax has taken your safety to heart. Big time."

Tessa looked at Walker, who clearly loved the attention of three women at once. The thought of him being a ladies man like his father crossed her mind, and she hated it. "Brax is concerned about his nephew. It's only right."

Claire frowned. "You're kidding. You think that's all he's worried about?"

"Seriously. I've seen the way he looks when he talks about you. He's just as concerned about you as he is about Walker—but in a different way." Maci shrugged. "It's the truth."

Suddenly, Tessa's knees felt weak. Could it be true? She collapsed into a seat at the kitchen table.

She wanted to believe them, to think that Brax cared about her. A few kisses were one thing. But deep, serious emotion? That was something else.

"I doubt Brax could ever trust me again after the way I lied," she confessed.

"Listen." Claire sat across from her, and she wasn't kidding anymore. "If there's one thing the Pattersons understand, it's survival. I mean, anybody would lie in your situation—so there's that right there. You had to be with Walker, but you didn't know what Robert had told Brax and whether Brax believed him."

Maci handed Walker to Claire, who looked like she was just about dying to hold him. "Those men respect people who do whatever it takes to survive. They're survivors. So are you. I know Brax respects you."

"Agreed." Claire beamed at the baby while bouncing him in her arms.

Were they right? She hoped so, since one thing was clearer every single day, and it scared her a little.

She was falling in love with Brax Patterson.

Chapter Twenty

If Brax had his choice of anybody in the world to work alongside, he would've chosen his brothers every time.

Things usually got intense when the stakes were high, but it had never been like this. For one thing, he was normally the one breaking the tension. Trying to pick up everybody's spirits, keeping the group from splintering due to emotions running high and hot.

Now? It was his brothers' turns to calm him.

"When I think of what could've happened…" He ran his hands through his hair before resting them on top of his head, almost like he was holding it in place. That was how it felt. Like his head might fall off because of everything going on inside.

"Here's an idea—stop thinking about it." Chance didn't bother softening this with a smile.

"He's right. You're driving yourself crazy." Luke patted Brax's shoulder on his way to the break room for fresh coffee.

Easy for them to say. Like he could let go of everything he'd seen and felt last night. There wasn't much in the world powerful enough to scare him. Last night qualified.

"But what if I'd been working late? What if it had been just Tessa and the baby at home? What if I hadn't been there?" He looked around the conference room, where they were working together to put a plan in place.

Weston blew out a long sigh. "It could've been much worse."

"What if we hadn't been awake at the time?" he continued, remembering the kisses in the kitchen, how sweet it had been to have Tessa in his arms. Close to him.

How right it had felt, bringing Walker downstairs for his feeding. How…satisfying. Like having a little family of his own. It had all fallen to pieces so fast. But like Weston had pointed out, it could've been so much worse.

Chance had his whiteboard out and the thing looked like some abstract masterpiece. Multicolored words and phrases scrawled everywhere. It was like he was planning an invasion.

Alibi. Witnesses. Testimony.

Brax's insides twisted at the sight of the word *alibi*. It referred to the iron-clad alibi Prince Riviera had presented to the cops during questioning. For both events. There'd been a dozen people hanging out together at that time of the morning. A dozen people willing and eager to offer proof of their late-night partying. How convenient.

And even if Prince had been partying like he'd

said, it didn't matter. He didn't have to be physically present at the scene for his thugs to do the dirty work for him—if anything, it was more likely that he would send them on ahead to keep his hands clean.

Like a man in his position ever had clean hands. He was the weakest, most cowardly one of them all.

Weston noticed Brax staring at the whiteboard. "You know, not a single cop in San Antonio believes a word that comes out of Riviera's mouth. Or his so-called associates."

Brax shook his head. "It doesn't do anybody on their hit list much good to know the police don't believe the bad guys. Not when there isn't enough evidence to tie said bad guys to anything. Doesn't make them any safer."

"Agreed. But law enforcement are on your side."

"I hope they still are when I need them again." Though if he had it his way, he wouldn't need them. Brax would take care of Prince Riviera on his own. With his bare hands if necessary.

Brax gladly accepted the fresh coffee Luke brought back for him. "Why is it that when we need to be our sharpest, it's usually when we're lacking sleep? Is it just me or is that the way it goes?"

Luke gave a one-shouldered shrug. "I know what you mean. You saw how I was when Claire was in the thick of it."

"As long as I make it through the next five days and get the pleasure of testifying against Riviera, at least one of my problems will be solved."

Luke didn't share Brax's hopeful grin. In fact, he

looked downright pained when he sat. He frowned at Brax. "I know this isn't what you want to hear, but do you think it's a good idea to look at the trial as the end of the road?"

"What do you mean?"

"I mean Riviera isn't the sort of guy who lets bygones be bygones. Let's say he goes to prison thanks to your testimony. You think he'll let it all go because he's behind bars? If anything, he'll be more determined than ever to get back at you."

The coffee went sour in Brax's mouth. Not that it had been all that great in the first place.

"Why didn't I think of that?" He looked around at his brothers as if any of them could give him an answer. "What's wrong with me?"

"There's nothing wrong with you. You're stretched thin, is all." Luke offered a slow nod. "I know what you're feeling. You can only think as far ahead as the solution for the most pressing problem you're facing at this moment."

"Think too far into the future and you're liable to think yourself into inertia—or madness," Weston added with a grim expression.

Unable to sit still, Brax jumped to his feet and paced the length of the room. "If I'm not safe after my testimony, that means Tessa and Walker won't be safe either. Not if they're anywhere near me."

It tore him up inside just thinking about them being in greater danger. Especially when he realized he was the reason for that danger. There was one thing he'd learned in the past twelve hours or so:

Tessa and Walker were his world, and he couldn't live without them.

"I think it's time we get the police department on this for real."

Brax turned toward Weston at his suggestion. "Meaning what?"

"Meaning we have them watch you. And Riviera. We'll know every move he makes, and we'll have eyes on you at all times to make sure you're okay. I think that's our best bet at the moment."

"You're probably right about that," Brax agreed. "I know I'd feel better if we had eyes on him and his associates." He rolled his eyes at that. *Associates.* Like the cartel was some sort of legitimate business.

"That doesn't change what might happen after you testify," Luke pointed out. "We need to think long-term."

"All right. Let's think long-term." Chance, always the strategist. He would be the one to jump on the idea of putting a plan together. "We can keep you hidden for a few years, if that's what it comes to. We have the resources. You could virtually vanish."

"Riviera's got connections, but there's no way he'd have enough to look for you all over the country," Luke mused. "It would be like looking for a needle in a haystack. He'd have to give up after a while, especially if the cartel implodes without him."

"Which is exactly what the DA is hoping will happen," Brax agreed. "His resources will only take him so far once he's inside, and the jackals will eat each other in his absence."

"But—"

They went silent. Weston drew a deep breath before continuing. "You'd have to go it alone. By yourself."

The implication hung heavy over their heads. No Tessa. No Walker.

On the one hand, he knew that was for the best. Riviera's thugs could still find him.

On the other hand, there was no other hand. He loathed the idea of being away from Tessa and Walker. What was the use of finding what he never knew he'd been waiting for if he ended up losing it so quickly?

"I don't know. This is a lot to process at once." He kept pacing like it would do any good, like it would help him make sense of the thoughts crashing into each other in his mind.

Saying goodbye to them or sticking around and exposing them to greater danger. They might not be so lucky next time, and he knew it.

He looked around the conference room. This was his business. These were his brothers. He was proud of what they'd built, just like they were. He didn't want to give up the results of their hard work. He couldn't abandon his brothers either. They were a team.

Not to mention the thought of losing Tessa and Walker completely gutted him.

"It's funny." He spoke more to himself than to any of them, looking at his feet as he walked the room. "For a minute there, I almost tricked myself into believing I had a normal life. Like this little game of house I've been playing with Tessa wasn't a game. It was comfortable. I felt normal."

"You are normal."

He chuckled at Weston without looking at him and replied, "Come on. You know what I mean."

"This won't be forever. You can have your normal life back once this blows over."

"I don't want to wait for it to blow over. I don't want to have to hide."

Luke snorted. Brax's head snapped around. "Is that funny?"

"Whoa, whoa." Luke held up his hands. "Don't shoot. I was reading a text from Claire. She's checking in from the apartment."

Brax scrubbed his hands over his face. "Sorry. I didn't—"

"It's okay."

He jerked his chin toward the phone. "What'd she say? How are things?"

"She says all is well over there. She and Maci dropped off the supplies."

"Great." That was one load off his mind, anyway. Maybe he'd overdone it with the list he'd given the women before sending them out, but Tessa and Walker's comfort meant too much for him to care.

"Claire likes her." Luke grinned. "And she thinks Walker's so cute she might want to reconsider her whole no-kids stance."

That got a laugh out of Brax. "She should've met him a few weeks back when all he could do was scream. Man, was it only a few weeks ago? It feels like a lifetime."

"A lot can happen in a month." Luke spread his arms. "Again, I know all about it."

A buzzing sound cut through the air, surprising them all. The front door normally wouldn't have been locked, but this wasn't a typical workday, and their office manager wasn't at the front desk to greet visitors. It had made sense to keep things locked up.

For that and for other reasons. Which was why they'd given Maci a little paid time off. If Riviera decided to pay a visit to the office...

Chance headed out there. "I'll see who it is."

"We don't get a lot of walk-ins, do we?" Luke asked, sitting up straighter than before, like he didn't trust the situation.

"Could be a delivery. Maci would have a better idea than we would of whether something was on its way." Weston started out like he wanted to back Chance up, but Chance's voice floated their way from the front door.

"Brax? Could you come out here?"

Brax looked at the others before going out to see what Chance wanted. He didn't sound panicked or even anxious. If anything, his voice had sounded... flat.

It took all of three seconds for Brax to understand why. The sight of somebody very familiar told him everything he needed to know.

"Hey, bro." Robert offered one of his typical greasy smiles. "Long time, no see."

Chapter Twenty-One

Brax rocked back on his heels. Not much in life had the power to render him speechless, but the sight of his lying, stealing, cheating, runaway half brother standing in front of him with the nerve to smile and act like nothing was wrong came pretty close.

Close enough to leave Brax at a loss for words.

Fortunately for him, he wasn't alone. "What do you think you're doing, showing up here like you didn't turn Brax's entire world upside down?" Chance demanded.

"Not just his world either," Luke muttered, dangerous and low, his hands curling into fists.

That made two of them—no, four of them, because a look around the entry area told Brax that all of his brothers wanted to take a swing at Robert.

Robert, meanwhile, glanced around and sighed. "Can we talk privately?" he asked Brax, ignoring the others.

Brax's blood only simmered harder than before. "If you have anything to say to me, you can say it in front of them."

Robert smirked. "Yeah, but you know how certain people are. Hot-blooded. Not able to listen to sense."

Weston's short, nearly silent hiss spoke volumes at Robert's racist comment. Brax lunged forward, taking Robert by his shirt collar and dragging him to the conference room. "You're lucky I need information from you, or else I'd let the three of them pull you apart while I watched and laughed."

"What's that supposed to mean?"

The fact that he could feign ignorance after his racist comment ratcheted Brax's fury to another level. He threw Robert into a chair and slammed the door behind them, knowing his brothers would be able to watch and listen to everything through the surveillance equipment installed in there. They'd probably be observing from Weston's office.

"So," he grunted while turning to face Robert. "What'd you come back for? You here to saddle me with more kids?"

The remark had its intended effect. Robert winced. "Hi to you too." He adjusted his clothes like Brax might've somehow hurt them.

Everything Robert did made Brax more inclined to kill him. His attitude, his racism, then preening like he was the injured party. Of all the nerve.

"People like you are good at playing the victim, aren't you?" Brax asked, forgetting everything else for the moment in favor of trying to understand his brother just a little.

"What do you mean?"

"If you can jump in and pretend to be hurt first,

you're deflecting from the problem at hand. It's how you go through your life, isn't it? Always trying to stay a step ahead, trying to distract people long enough so that they won't have the opportunity to kill you for the harm you've caused."

Something flickered in Robert's eyes. Something like understanding. Maybe even fear.

It cleared quickly. "I don't know what you're talking about."

"Of course, you don't." Brax pulled out a chair. "You have a lot of explaining to do."

The trick to this little interrogation would be avoiding the topic of Tessa. He couldn't let Robert know she was back in Walker's life or that he'd even met her. Tessa was supposed to be dead, according to the little story Robert had told, and if Brax had any hope of prying the truth from somebody so disassociated from truth, it would mean stepping carefully.

A shame, since it would've been gratifying to see him sweat over the legal ramifications of falsified documents.

But no, what mattered more was Tessa. If Robert contacted CPS and they took Walker away from her again, it would break her. Brax had no doubt.

He glanced up at one of the discreet cameras mounted in the corner of the room. They'd be watching.

It was Robert who spoke first. "I want Walker back."

Brax whirled on him. This was the last thing he'd expected. An explanation, maybe. A sob story, likely. But this?

"What are you talking about? You had the paperwork drawn up and everything. Is this some kind of a game to you?"

"Things have changed." How the man could sit there, unblinking, and deliver such a load of...

Brax shook his head. "That doesn't matter. You don't drag the law into something and then up and change your mind. What gives?"

Robert didn't respond.

Brax took a chair, straddled it, facing his brother. "I mean it. Fess up. What's this really about?"

"I told you. Things have changed." Only now he was shifting slightly in his chair. Uncomfortable.

Brax decided to press harder on that uncomfortable spot. "You just decided you want your son back? After awarding me guardianship? It doesn't seem like the sort of decision a person randomly changes their mind about."

"It wasn't random."

"So why, then? Why is he suddenly convenient to your life?"

Robert rolled his eyes with a heavy, put-on sigh. "I miss the little guy. He's my son. Isn't it right that I miss him? I mean, you're the moral authority. You tell me."

Brax snorted. "Moral authority? Fine. I'll give you moral authority—you can't pass your kid off like an inconvenient house plant whenever you feel like it, then decide you made a mistake and want him back. I know he's just a baby, but it's not good for him to lose his routine like that. You've already done it once.

Now, he's in a routine with a nanny he likes." That was as much as he could admit about Tessa.

"You just said it yourself. He's a baby." Robert drew this out like he was talking to one just then. "It doesn't matter yet. He won't remember any of this."

"Because you're an expert in child development now?"

"Are you?"

"You might be surprised what I've had to learn on the fly," Brax murmured, holding Robert's gaze. "When a few days turned into this many weeks."

"Okay, okay, I admit I lost my head a little." Robert sat back, hands in the air. "It happens to everybody. I couldn't see myself making it work. I figured I was no good for the kid and you would be a better parent. I mean, look at you. All settled into your fancy office and your bros out there."

"Watch it," Brax warned, always aware of those cameras.

"But I changed my mind," Robert continued. So intense, like he believed himself.

Not that it mattered.

"You can't change your mind. What about this isn't getting through to you? What happens if you decide to change your mind again? That's not how this works."

"Where is he?" Robert's eyes narrowed. "I went to the house but it was empty. It looked like there was a fire there."

Brax's jaw tightened. What would've happened if there hadn't been a fire and Tessa had been at the house with Walker when Robert had showed up? The thought made him sick.

"He's somewhere else, with the nanny. They're doing fine. The fire was just an accident, but it didn't spread beyond the living room."

"That's good to hear. I hate to think of my son being in danger."

"Accidents happen," Brax muttered, teeth clenched at the nerve of the man in front of him. "He's perfectly safe and happy right now."

"Where's he staying?"

"Why does it matter when I have legal guardianship and you don't? You handed him over to me, and I take that seriously. When you decide to float in and out of his life, I have to question why."

Robert laughed. "I'd think you would be happy to be free of him. No more daddy duty. You should be thanking me!"

Brax held onto the arms of the chair to keep from throwing a punch. "I'm pretty happy with the way things turned out, actually. Sorry if you thought I'd throw the kid at you and run in the other direction, but that's not how this is going down."

Robert swallowed, eyes darting back and forth over Brax's face like he was trying to sense whether this was a game or not.

It was like magic. Robert deflated bit by bit. The shoulders slumped. His mouth tugged downward at the corners into something like a sad clown's grimace. He slouched in the chair.

"I need him back."

They were getting closer to the truth, finally. "Why? Why now? What changed?"

"There's people after me. Bad people."

What a big surprise. Brax glanced at one of the cameras, knowing what his brothers would be thinking then. It took long enough for him to admit what they'd known for days, ever since Tessa had revealed all.

"That's all the more reason to leave Walker with me, isn't it? To protect him from the people after you?"

"It's not like that."

"Are you kidding? How else could it possibly be? You're in danger. Why would you want to bring your son back into it?"

Robert shook his head, looking at the floor. "It's complicated."

"When is it not?" Brax leveled his gaze, staring straight at Robert. "Who are these people?"

He drew a deep breath and let it out slowly before answering. "The Solomon family."

Brax rocked back for the second time that day. He hadn't expected this. "The family that owns casinos all over the country? That Solomon family?"

"Yes."

"They're insanely wealthy."

"I know."

"And you got on their bad side? I mean, I can see rubbing elbows with them, but you'd have to be a real idiot—"

"Okay, okay. I don't need the insults."

Brax gritted his teeth. It was one thing to be a professional gambler, but to get on a casino owner's hit list? It took a special kind of stupid to cross a family with that kind of power and influence.

"Do you owe them money?" It was the easiest guess.

Robert nodded. "Yeah. That was the money I was trying to scratch together when I left Walker with you."

"Right."

Still, Robert stared at the floor, fingers picking at the armrests. There was more to the story. "What else? This isn't all about money. Don't bother lying and wasting my time."

A heavy sigh. "I was sort of involved with a member of the family."

For the sake of everything. "Okay."

"Gabrielle Solomon. She was visiting the Eagle Pass casino. I don't know if you've ever seen her, but she's hot. And smart. Into the business side of things, not just spending the family money. I couldn't keep my eyes off her."

Or his hands, Brax would've bet.

"The first time I talked to her, she told me she loves kids. Babies, you know. I told her I had a kid. She lit up."

A sick certainty started unfurling in Brax's gut, but he needed to hear it from Robert. He wouldn't let him off the hook.

Robert lifted a shoulder. "So I played up the single-dad thing. She fell in love with Walker, and it brought us closer."

Which was why he'd stolen Walker away from
Tessa. So he could seduce some wealthy woman,
who might've been smart, but wasn't smart enough
to see through him.

If there had ever been a time Brax wanted to kill
Robert, this was it. All the agony he'd put Tessa
through, and all so he could rope a woman.

"I screwed things up," Robert admitted, rubbing
his temples. "I was so stupid. I cheated on her."

"On Gabrielle Solomon?"

"Just the one time. A couple nights before I went
to you. She threw a fit, told me she's not the sort of
woman guys cheat on and get away with it. Threw
me out. She told her brother Victor, and he decided
all the money I owed them was due immediately."

"Do I even want to know how much?"

Robert cringed. "Fifty thousand."

Brax closed his eyes for a moment as this washed
over him.

"I've been running from them ever since. I don't
know what I'm going to do." Robert shrugged before
bending forward, resting his elbows on his knees and
his face in his hands.

Brax thought it over for a little while before pointing out, "They're not going to kill you, if that's what
you're worried about. That's not how they'll get their
money back. If I were you, I'd go back and take my
beating, then work out a plan."

When Robert flinched, Brax added, "I know
it's easier said than done, but they won't let this go.

Would you rather live on the run for the rest of your life?"

"Well…"

"Don't tell me there's more to this."

"One of the guys on their security team…hates me. It's personal."

"What does that mean?"

"I said some things back in the day, he took it the wrong way. Overly sensitive," he scoffed.

Brax rolled his eyes. "What's his name?"

"Jakob Hawkins. He wants to kill me."

"Robert."

He looked up, his face hard. "He does. When he finds me, he's going to kill me. He's made that clear to everybody he knows."

"And you thought what? Get Walker back and make up with Gabrielle? Or use him as a human shield, hoping this Jakob would change his mind when he saw the baby? That was your big plan? What if this Jakob found you and killed you anyway? What would happen to your son?"

Robert had no answer for that, which hardly came as a surprise. Brax knew he hadn't thought about his son, not really. Walker's future meant nothing when compared to Robert getting himself out of the latest crisis.

No way would Brax let that happen. Robert wasn't about to get his hands on Walker, not ever again. Even if he hadn't known about the history with CPS and Tessa, this situation on its surface was more than enough for Brax to keep Walker as far from his father as possible.

Still, the longer the Solomon family was after Robert, the longer they'd be after Tessa. He couldn't let that continue. Especially since they'd asked her where Walker was when they'd threatened her in the mall parking lot.

Did they want to use Walker as a pawn to get to Robert?

Brax wouldn't let that happen either.

"Well, I don't have the money, if you were wondering." Brax stood. "But I think there might be something I could do for you."

Robert's eyes lit up. "What's that?"

"Give me forty-eight hours. I was lying about the nanny having Walker right now. My parents do, and they're out of town. It'll take time to get him."

"Your parents?" Robert scoffed. "Great. I hope they don't take him out anywhere, or people might wonder."

Brax's patience snapped. "What's that supposed to mean?"

"Hey, hey!" Robert held up his hands in mock self-defense. "I'm not the one saying it. I just bet other people are, is all. Like why are they out with a little white kid? You need to get a sense of humor."

He grinned on his way out of the conference room. "See you in forty-eight hours, bro."

It took every scrap of self-control not to break Robert's head open. He waited until he heard the front door open and close before leaving the room.

Weston's office door opened at the same time, and his brothers filed out. They didn't say a word about Robert's comments, though the set of their jaws made words unnecessary.

Chance cleared his throat. "Weston found information on this Jakob Hawkins." He nodded toward the laptop Weston had brought with him.

One look at the photo on the screen was enough. "That's the guy. I recognize the pockmarked skin."

"Now we probably have a good idea why he hates Robert so much," Luke muttered. Everything about him screamed tension, from his voice to his folded arms.

"Yeah, imagine the sort of so-called jokes Robert made at his expense." Brax's lip curled in disgust. "You have no idea how much of me wants to let him get what's coming to him, but as long as he's on the run and they're not finding him—"

"It affects Tessa," Weston confirmed.

Brax sank into a chair and blew out a long breath while looking at the ceiling. There were bits and pieces of a plan moving around in his head, but it was still shadowy. Sketchy. He didn't have much time to solidify things.

"Do you think the Solomon family itself want Robert dead?" Chance posed. "Is this coming from them, or is it strictly because Hawkins hates Robert and wants an excuse?"

"The Solomons are rich," Brax mused. "But not stupid. And they're powerful, but they're not a crime family per se. I don't know whether murder is in their bag of tricks, but wouldn't we know if it was? Word spreads."

"Odds are they don't care one way or another about Robert," Chance decided. "The money is a drop in the bucket. A lot to us, but nothing to them. They probably wouldn't blink an eye if he ended up dead. Especially after he cheated on Gabrielle."

"An honor thing," Weston muttered. "But if they'd put their money behind finding Robert, he'd be dead by now. No question. This sounds like Hawkins and a buddy of his working on their own."

"Not to rain on anybody's parade, but you have bigger problems than this Hawkins guy being after Robert." Chance offered a shrug when Brax looked his way. "Prince Riviera?"

"Of course, but this Hawkins might be a threat to Tessa, and I can't let him hurt her. I can deal with the cartel after I know she's in the clear. Besides, there's still the idea of me having to go away. I don't want to, but if things come down to that, I'll need to know Tessa and Walker are free of Robert forever. I couldn't stand it otherwise."

He stood, slid his hands into his pockets, and looked at his brothers. "I have a plan."

He turned to Weston. "I think you were right about involving the police in this. Can you call some of your old colleagues with the San Antonio PD?"

Chapter Twenty-Two

Tessa jumped like a skittish rabbit when the key turned in the lock on the front door.

Brax had texted to let her know he was leaving for the apartment, with two of his brothers following him. Then he'd texted to tell her he was in the garage and on his way up.

Even with his thoughtful warnings, she couldn't breathe until he opened the door and poked his head into the living room.

Then, it was like her feet had a mind of their own. She closed the distance between them before she knew what was happening.

She stopped short before she could do anything stupid. What if he didn't want her to jump all over him like an overexcited puppy the minute he walked through the door?

The flash of his smile told her otherwise. He pulled her into a hug, wrapping her up tight. He filled her world. Pressed against him, she could forget about everything for a little while.

"Hi," he murmured against the top of her head before planting a kiss there. "How's it going?"

"Would it be too unforgivably corny if I said it's going better now that you're here?"

Laughter rumbled in his chest up against her ear. "Corny, but not unforgivably."

"Good." She snuggled closer, breathing in his scent, drinking in his warmth. "How are you?"

"Not the worst I've ever been. Not anymore." He pulled back enough to look down at her. How would he feel about staring at each other this way for the rest of their lives?

If being held in his arms was balm for her wounded soul, his kiss was nothing short of heaven. His arms tightened. A groan from the back of his throat awakened something deep in her core. This was all she needed—this and her son.

The three of them. What if this could be their life?

Not this, exactly. The thought of it pulled her back to reality. They were standing in a safe house because she was hiding from all sorts of bad guys. No, she didn't want this exact situation to be her life.

She smiled when the kiss was over, standing on tiptoe to brush her nose against his. "Did you eat?"

"Not yet. I'll dig up something."

"You'll do no such thing. Let me. You look so tired." He followed her toward the kitchen, stopping to check the bedroom where Walker slept before joining her.

"How was your day? I see you're good and stocked up now."

"It was sweet of Maci and Claire to go out and shop. And sweet of you to make them a list."

"It's the least I could do."

Tessa didn't exactly agree. She was in this apartment thanks to him. She had her son thanks to him.

"Claire and Maci are great. It's been a long time since I chatted with the girls. They made me feel like we were old friends." She couldn't suppress a grin.

"I knew you would get along." He smiled, too, but she'd been right. He did look tired. The overhead light made the circles under his eyes more prominent.

She stopped making his sandwich to touch his scruffy cheek. "You really do need some rest. I'm starting to become a little worried about you."

"This is nothing. You've never seen me exhausted. I'm only slightly tired right now."

"I know you think you're helping your cause, but you aren't."

"I'm the last thing you need to worry about. I've been handling myself for a long time."

"I need you to know I'm here for you." He smiled in an indulgent, "aren't you cute" sort of way. "Seriously," she insisted. "So far, you've been super involved in my problems. I want you to know I'm here for you. This goes both ways. It can't be all me, me, me."

"I don't see you that way. I never would."

"Well, thank you, but you get what I mean." She turned to him, plate in hand, and it was plain he leaned against the wall to prop himself up. "Come on. Let's sit in the living room where you can be more comfortable."

He joined her on the couch, kicking off his shoes

with a sigh before taking the huge sandwich she'd fixed. "My favorite." He grinned, taking in the sight of the turkey, Swiss cheese, coleslaw and Russian dressing on rye.

"Maci told me it's what you always order when she goes for sandwiches. She figured she'd buy the ingredients in case you had a hankering."

"She's a godsend." He closed his eyes after taking a bite and groaned. "Oh, yeah."

"That good, huh?"

"Sometimes a simple thing like this really hits the spot." He looked genuinely happy while devouring the sandwich in far fewer bites than Tessa could have managed.

She sat facing him, legs crossed in front of her. "So now that you've gorged, can you tell me what's going on? Share a little something with me? I know bad guys are after you, but I'll go nuts without updates on anything new."

"I appreciate you caring." He leaned over, leaving the plate and napkin on the coffee table, then sank back against the cushions with a sigh. "I don't want to burden you."

"It's not a burden."

He shot her a knowing look, stopping just short of rolling his eyes.

"Even if it is a burden, that's fine. I have pretty strong shoulders." She wiggled them around, hoping to get a smile from him.

And she did, though it was brief.

"I know you're a strong person." His hand found hers. "But you've already handled so much."

"I can handle more. Please. Let me in. Tell me what's happening."

He let out a long breath, puffing out his cheeks. "Okay. It's not going to be easy."

She braced herself.

His hand tightened. "Robert's back in town. He came to the office today. He wants Walker back."

Her head snapped back. Her body went into panic mode: heart racing, blood roaring in her ears, her stomach in knots, muscles twitching. She had to move. She had to leave before Robert found her.

Before he took Walker away from her again.

"Hey, hey." Brax moved closer until she was practically in his lap. "It's going to be okay. Just because he's back doesn't mean he'll get Walker. That's not going to happen."

"I…" She looked away from him because his face was so earnest, and she liked looking at it so much, but she was going to have to leave. How could she leave him?

"I know what you're thinking right now." With his free hand, he cupped the back of her head and drew her close, touching his forehead to hers. "I get it. I do. Just breathe. No way in hell am I or my brothers—my real brothers—going to let that happen. You can trust me on that, okay? We will never let him take Walker away."

She breathed the way he'd asked her to, and after a few minutes, was calm enough to ask, "How? He has documents on his side. Even if they're fake, it'll take time to prove they are, and in the meantime, he could take the baby and go anywhere. What if he runs and is never found?"

"I'm telling you. We're not going to let that happen. He won't so much as put his hands on Walker."

"No offense, but how can you be so certain?"

"I have a plan."

Hope stirred in her still-racing heart.

He continued, "We'll get it on record that Robert went through illegal channels to take the baby from you. That he falsified information. Once that's done, you'll get full custody back. The Patterson brothers are going to make sure of it."

It was so easy to believe him because she wanted to believe. She wanted what he said to be true with every ounce of her being.

That didn't mean she missed his choice of words.

"The Patterson brothers will make sure of it?" She pulled back just enough to look him in the eye, searching for answers.

"Right."

"Not you, personally?" She narrowed her eyes at him. "I'm not saying you have to do it all yourself. But you've always made it sound like you were the one fighting for me and Walker. Why shift it to your brothers now? What am I missing?"

The way his brows drew together spoke volumes. So she was right. Brax Patterson wasn't exactly an open book, but she'd learned enough about him to know how he operated.

He took the situation with her and Walker seriously. Personally. He might rely on his brothers for help, but he would never straight up outsource.

"Things are getting more dangerous with Riviera and the cartel. You of all people know that." He stroked her hair, looking deep into her eyes. "I might have to go off the grid for a while because of it. I won't do it until you're completely in the clear. I swear it."

Her chest ached. Her throat went tight.

He was leaving her.

Maybe he had never been with her in the first place.

Sure, those few kisses had been mind-blowing, but that was all they had. No promises.

She sat up straighter, patting the hand on the back of her head. He let it fall away. "So you're going away to keep yourself safe. That's smart. It's what I would want you to do. Those guys—"

"Tessa—"

"—Those guys won't stop until they shut you up. I mean, it won't be easy on you."

"Would you listen to me?"

She tried to turn away, to reposition herself on the couch so he couldn't see the emotion she fought against. The disappointment crushing her insides.

He wasn't having it. "Listen, please." Taking her by the shoulders, he turned her to him. "Do you think I'm trying to run away from you? Nothing could be further from the truth. Don't you know by now how much I want to be part of your life? Not just Walker's life, but yours. I want us to be together. But not if it means putting you in jeopardy. You are my number one concern right now. Do you believe me?"

There was no other way to answer. "Yes."

"Good."

"So what's your plan?"

He shot her a rueful smile. "Funny you should ask, since it involves you. Don't worry," he was quick to add at her sharp intake of breath. "It's nothing huge. You don't have to show your face, and you don't have to even speak to Robert. For the record, he has no idea you're even in town, and we're going to keep it that way."

"Okay." But her voice sounded shaky even to her.

"I'm going to need you to call that guy. The one who tracked you down. We have his name now, thanks to Robert, and his contact information. Don't bother asking."

Her mouth snapped shut, because she'd been about to ask how they managed it. The Pattersons had their ways.

"You'll call him and tell him you know where Robert is. That's all you have to do. My brothers and I and the police will handle the rest. If all goes as planned—and there's no reason it shouldn't—both Robert and this Jakob Hawkins who's been terrorizing you will be arrested. And you'll be free."

"Free." The word fell from her lips like a prayer. It felt foreign, like a language she hadn't learned yet.

"That's what I want for you." He kissed her forehead, her cheeks. "I want you to be free and to feel safe. You deserve nothing less than the whole world.

I might not be able to give you the whole world, but I can give you this."

And she would accept it gladly, though she wanted more. She wanted the man whose arms she was now in. The man who would put his plans to keep himself safe from the cartel on hold to ensure she was taken care of first.

He was her miracle. Everything she could ever want.

She kissed him, melting into his arms. She kissed him over and over. Every time their mouths met, she only wanted more. Like a thirst that got worse the more she drank.

She'd never have enough.

He held back a little, eventually pulling his head away and taking her by the shoulders, holding her in place. "You don't have to do this. You don't owe me anything."

She ran her hands over his arms, his shoulders. "I know that."

"It's just that I don't want you to feel like you don't have a choice."

Her hands moved to his face, one on either side. She stroked his scruffy cheeks with her thumbs and wondered what she'd ever done to deserve a man like him in her life. Before meeting Brax, she'd had no idea men like him existed.

There was so much concern in his eyes. It was almost enough to break her heart, the way he cared about her.

"I know I have a choice," she whispered, and she meant it with all her heart. "And I choose you."

A soft smile touched the corners of his mouth before he pulled her in, and this time there was no hesitation as his mouth crushed against hers and his arms held her tight against his unyielding chest.

His heart pounded there—she felt it when her hand slid over his chest, then up under his shirt as she worked it over his head.

Her heart pounded too. But for once, it wasn't fear. Fear was the last thing on her mind as Brax lowered her to the couch and stretched out on top of her, wiping away all thoughts of anything but him. And her. Together.

Chapter Twenty-Three

Time had never moved so slowly. Brax was certain of it.

"One hour." As if Chance needed to announce it. Like Brax hadn't looked at the time every few minutes since they'd arrived at the office.

"And Robert knows where you're supposed to be meeting him?" Tessa asked, standing at Brax's side. They had been joined at the hip the past two days.

Not that he would've complained for anything, since it had been the happiest two days he'd ever spent. There hadn't been anything in the world but her and Walker.

Mostly her. They hadn't been able to keep their hands off each other since that first night together, which had resulted in two days of jumping in and out of bed.

And the couch. And once on the kitchen counter, but that had been completely spontaneous.

Now, she was more precious to him than ever. He would've done anything for this woman who'd become his world. The fact that this would involve putting his useless half brother behind bars was gravy at that point.

He clasped her hand, squeezing once to reassure her. "He does. He said he's familiar with the area. An old warehouse just outside of town."

"Why would he be familiar with that?"

"Who knows?" Chance shrugged. "There could've been any number of illegal activities going on out there. Gambling, drugs, you name it. Robert isn't exactly discriminating when it comes to how he gets his fix."

"What bothered me was how glad he sounded when I told him where to meet," Brax admitted. "Once he knew it would be an empty place, he seemed relieved."

"What could that mean?" Tessa looked around the room.

Chance pursed his lips, his brow furrowing. "He's suspicious, maybe? Then again, somebody who's left nothing but havoc in his wake for so long is bound to be suspicious by nature."

"Don't worry. I'll do whatever it takes to calm him and get him talking." He squeezed Tessa's hand again, and the smile she offered went a long way toward easing his concerns for her.

She was handling this like a champ. He should've known she would. The pride he felt when he looked at her knew no bounds.

"You ready to make the call?" Chance asked.

She responded with a firm nod, her jaw tight. "Absolutely."

Her hand didn't so much as tremble as she punched in Jakob's number. The phone's speaker was turned on so they could all hear what he had to say and could coach Tessa through any sudden changes in the script.

Brax caught her eye as the phone rang. *You can do this*, he mouthed, giving her a thumbs up. She stood a little straighter, nodding once.

"Yeah?" The voice rang out in the conference room.

Tessa lifted her chin. "Jakob Hawkins?"

"Yeah, this is him. Don't tell me. Tessa?"

"You know my voice?" Her lips pursed.

"I do. Although I never thought you would be the one reaching out to me. What's this about?"

Her tongue darted out over her lips. "I know where Robert is, and I figured I should pass the information on to you."

Right, right, stick to the script. Brax nodded, hoping to encourage her.

"Oh, really?"

"Yes, really. I told you before that I didn't know, and that was the truth. But he's in town again, and I know where he's going to be exactly one hour from now. I thought you'd want to know."

"I got to admit, you've piqued my interest."

"Not so fast. I want a little something for my trouble. You've put me through the wringer, and I deserve at least a little something."

"What did you have in mind?"

Brax prayed this would work.

"A thousand dollars," Tessa announced, closing her eyes briefly when she said it. Brax had settled on this amount, thinking it was enough to make her sound serious but not so much that Hawkins would balk at the number.

"Sounds good to me. As long as I can get my hands on that loser." He paused. "Where's he going to be?"

"There's a warehouse outside of town. He's meeting somebody there." She rattled off the directions as Brax had written them down.

"So he'll be in the middle of nowhere is what you're telling me."

"I'm only telling you what I know."

"Who's he meeting?"

Tessa glanced at Brax. "Like I said, that's all I know. That he'll be there in an hour."

"You expect me to walk into a situation without knowing who I'm going to find there? No way, baby. I'm going to need a little more than that."

Brax shook his head, making sure Tessa saw him when he did it. No way was he going to let this scum set the terms.

"Like what?" she asked. Brax shook his head harder, waving his hands back and forth in a "no way" motion.

"Like you meeting me there."

Chance held Brax's arm, signaling him to stay quiet. It was easy for him, wasn't it? If Luke had been there, he might get it, but he and Claire were at the safe house with Walker.

To his horror, Tessa asked, "And what would happen once you see Robert there, just like I promised?"

"You'd be free to go. I don't need anything from you but a little bit of insurance. I'm not walking into some empty warehouse without knowing I'm covered."

Brax vibrated with rage. Was he supposed to stand back and let this happen? How could he live with himself if Tessa got hurt? Or worse. Why would she want to breathe the same air as this scum?

"Okay," she agreed, and Brax gritted his teeth against the torrent that threatened to pour out. Every filthy word he'd ever learned wanted to make itself heard, plus a few that might not have existed.

"Meet you there," Hawkins promised before ending the call.

Brax managed to wait until a series of beeps signaled the line had gone dead before exploding. "Why would you do that? Why would you agree to anything he asked?"

Her eyes went wide, her mouth falling open in surprise. "Because he wouldn't have gone if I wasn't going to be there. Weren't you listening?"

"You never let the target dictate the terms, Tessa. I don't want you going anywhere near him."

"Do you think I want to be near him? This isn't something I'm looking forward to, you know."

"Okay, you two." Chance tried to get in between them, but all Tessa did was sidestep so she could continue glaring at Brax like he was the bad guy.

"I'll do anything to keep Walker safe. Got it?" she asked, hands on her hips. "Don't ask me not to do whatever it takes. If showing my face is going to get Hawkins to relax and believe Robert's there and he isn't in any danger, that's fine by me."

"It's a solid plan," Chance reminded him. "Weston's already out there with Rick and his guys. We've wired the entire warehouse, and you'll be wearing a wire and recording every word Robert says. The cops will pick up Robert and Hawkins a couple miles from the warehouse. And I'll be outside watching Tessa. Once Hawkins leaves with Robert, I'll follow and keep Hawkins from killing him before they reach the police."

Brax nodded. "Right, right. I know that. But there was a plan in place for this call, wasn't there? And here we are, going completely off-script. I don't want Tessa there."

"You might want to try not talking about me as if I am not here," Tessa suggested, raising an eyebrow.

He scrubbed his hands over his head, at a loss. "You know it's not like that. I'm not trying to talk around you or like you don't matter. If you didn't matter, I wouldn't be so against you getting yourself wrapped up in this."

"Newsflash—" she went to him, looping her arms around his waist "—I'm wrapped up in it. I'll show my face, Hawkins will trust Robert is inside, and that'll be it."

"Come on. We'd better get moving." Chance motioned for them to follow him outside.

Brax knew there was nothing more he could do. No time. The plan was already in motion. He had to be there before Robert showed up.

They walked outside together, hand in hand. "Listen to me, please," he urged on the way to the car. "You can't get too close to Hawkins. Play your part, show your face, then get out of there. Okay?"

"Okay."

"You promise?" He turned to her, taking her precious face into his hands. She would never understand how important she was. How her well-being meant more to him than his own. Why, if it seemed like he came down too hard on her, it was done out of love.

"I promise." She covered his hands with hers, smiling. "Hey. After all I've been through to be with my baby, to be with him without looking over my shoulder, do you honestly think I'd risk getting killed? Risk leaving him alone? No way. I promise you I will play it safe."

He kissed her once, firmly, before letting her go. There would be time for everything else later. He could show her and tell her everything she meant to him. How his life had meaning now thanks to her and Walker. How he'd waited so long without knowing he was waiting, because he could never have imagined somebody like her existed.

Somebody so perfect for him. So perfect in general.

As long as she stuck to her word and Hawkins didn't decide to do something crazy, he'd have the opportunity to tell her everything he held in his heart.

Chapter Twenty-Four

"Weston. Come in." Brax adjusted the earpiece, setting it deep inside his ear.

"I hear you, brother. Loud and clear. ETA?"

Brax checked the GPS on the console. "Five minutes."

"Great. We're ready and waiting out here. You know what you're doing once he shows?"

"I've been through it a hundred times in my head, beginning to end. Believe me."

"Remind me anyway."

Brax rolled his eyes. Weston, ever the cop. "I have to get Robert to confess to what he did. Trust me. I know. I have my wire, and there's recording equipment all over the warehouse. Chance will watch the exterior. Tessa will meet Hawkins outside the warehouse so he knows—"

"Tessa?"

Right. He didn't know. "Believe me. I don't want her involved. Hawkins insisted she show her face so he'd know she wasn't lying."

"Wonderful. I should have guessed he wouldn't let it go that easily."

"I have to get as much information from Hawkins as possible. He has to admit he's been tracking Robert because he intends to kill him. I'm telling you, I'm on it."

"All right. Just checking. We have everything covered on our end, as well. You focus on your part, and we'll take care of the rest."

Sure. It would be easy.

Brax didn't believe it for a second. Nothing about this went easy. Ever.

Then again, maybe this meant they were due a little good luck. It would certainly be welcome.

He reached the warehouse a minute earlier than the GPS had predicted. He'd beaten everybody else, which was a good thing. The car seat was in the back, and he made a big deal of unloading it and carrying it into the warehouse.

He even talked to the doll and bundle of blankets inside, just in case Robert was watching from somewhere nearby. Not that he'd give Robert credit for thinking that far ahead, but anomalies happened, and now would be the worst time to get caught in a lie.

He had barely stepped foot inside when Chance's voice rang out in his ear. "He's coming. Just about to reach the warehouse."

Brax took one deep breath after another, forcing himself to relax. Telling himself he was there to give the baby to Robert—the way he was supposed to be.

That he cared about his half brother and only wanted what was best for him.

A sick joke, but one he had to at least pretend to believe if he had any hope of coming off believable.

"We're a go," Weston announced. "You've got this, Brax."

"Yeah, and now I just have to figure out what to do with it." The fact that he could make a joke had to be a good sign. He hoped.

Robert stepped through the open door, his head sweeping from side to side. "I had half an idea you brought me here to set me up," he giggled like a little girl once he found they were alone.

"This is too serious for anything like that."

Robert shrugged. "So? Hand him over."

Brax took a step back. "Not until you tell me how things turned out this way. You're still my brother. I can't let you walk out of my life again without knowing how you got into this situation. And what you plan on doing after this."

"Why does it matter all of a sudden?"

"Call me sentimental. Now more than ever, since I happen to have formed an attachment to your son. I want to know what his father's planning on doing after he leaves this warehouse."

That greasy smile. "I'm gonna stay alive, bro. You know me. Always one step ahead of the bad guys."

Brax withheld comment. He had to keep things moving in the right direction, ideally before Hawkins showed up. "You said Walker's mother is dead? Is that true? Be honest with me now, please. This might be the last time we see each other for all I know. I think after you dropped your kid on my doorstep and disappeared, you owe me that much."

Robert's eye roll was visible from the open door and the dim light filtering through the few filthy windows lining the walls. "What do you want me to say? She was a loser. She didn't know how to handle herself, much less our kid."

Brax stopped short of snarling, but just barely. "It doesn't say much about you that you were hooking up with a loser who couldn't handle herself."

"She was cute. What can I say? Anyway, she was no good, so I got custody."

"You must've had proof of her being no good. Judges don't up and grant custody to a professional gambler—no offense—over a baby's mother."

"Like her being a waitress at a casino was any better?" Robert scoffed. "Please. It took no time. My cousin, you remember. He's a judge."

He was making it so easy, it was hard not to laugh. "Oh, so it was like that? You got him to fix things for you?"

"Listen, Brax. Don't get up on your moral high horse now. I did what I needed to do."

"What does that mean? Did you steal this baby from his mother? Does she even know what's going on with you and the Solomon family?"

"No, why would she? For all I know she's in a hole somewhere. What does it matter? The important thing is I got Walker and that's that."

"Even though you had to lie to do it?"

"What do you want me to say? Yeah. I did what had to be done. I had my cousin fix things. He told me what to tell CPS, what they would listen to, and I told them. Bing, bang, boom, I got full custody of my son."

"You lied to Child Protective Services?" Always good to have clear confirmation.

"Yes, okay? I told them she was an addict and fixed it so CPS would show up while she was high on something. She didn't even know I had a buddy inject her as she was leaving work that night. I called CPS and had them go to her place, and they saw with their own eyes what a waste she was. It was easy after that."

He had just signed his own arrest warrant. Brax took pains to calm himself. "And the judge who helped you get away with it is the same cousin who accepted my forged signature on those guardianship documents?"

Robert sighed. "Why do you have to make it sound the way you do? 'Forged.' I mean, come on."

"I never signed those guardianship documents, yet he approved and signed them. He granted me guardianship sight unseen."

"He knew you're my half brother."

"It doesn't matter. I never met him, yet he was on board with doctoring those papers."

"This is a waste of my time. I should've known it wouldn't be enough for you to hand the kid over and be done with it. You had to let me know what a scumbag you think I am and how much you hate me."

"I don't hate you," Brax insisted. "I feel sorry for you, if anything."

"Spare me your pity." Robert strode over to him, hands out. "I need the kid. I have places to be."

"Brax?" Chance murmured in his ear. "Tessa and Hawkins are on their way in."

Perfect timing.

Brax handed the car seat to Robert, watching with pleasure as his expression changed from snide arrogance to confusion. "What is this?" He peeled back the blankets, revealing the doll in Walker's place. "What do you think you're doing?"

"I'm protecting people who aren't scum," Brax fired back.

A moment later, Hawkins walked in with Tessa behind him. Robert's mouth fell open. He dropped the seat, the sound echoing in the empty space.

He turned to Brax, snarling. "What have you done?"

Meanwhile, Hawkins let out a satisfied breath. "You were as good as your word." He turned to Tessa with a grin. "Thank you. And sorry for all the trouble I put you through. You can go." He handed her a fat envelope.

Tessa withdrew a wad of cash from the envelope, counted it and exchanged a look with Brax before glaring at Robert. She didn't say a word, only stood there with her arms wrapped around herself, hate burning in her eyes.

Brax let out a relieved breath when she backed out of the warehouse. A moment later, Chance reported, "She's safe. She's cleared the building and gone to her car."

Robert turned on Brax, sweating like he'd just run a marathon. "Why would you do this to your own brother?" he snarled.

"You stole your son from his mother and used him as a pawn," Brax snarled back. He didn't have to pretend anymore. "You did everything you could to destroy her. How am I supposed to have sympathy for you? You deserve everything you're going to get."

"I agree." Hawkins advanced, but Brax held up a hand to stop him. This wasn't over yet.

"You can't get the money he owes the Solomon family if you kill him," Brax reminded him.

Hawkins shrugged, then took Robert by his shirt collar and drove a fist into his face once, twice. Robert dropped to the floor.

Hawkins turned to Brax. "If you wanted your brother alive, you shouldn't have brought him to me. You probably know better than most how much he deserves to die—hell, what you just said now about his kid is reason enough. I've got my own personal issues with Robert."

He kicked Robert in the ribs to punctuate his statement. "Don't I?" he shouted, the sudden change making Brax jump. "I warned you I'd kill you if you didn't quit saying the things you were saying. Making a fool out of me. Then you made a fool of the family. Of Gabrielle. That was all the reason I needed to go after you. They know I'm gonna kill you, Robert, and guess what? They don't care as long as they never have to set eyes on you again."

A chill ran through Brax.

Weston broke in. "That's all the police need. We'll pick them up once they're out of there. Chance will follow them."

"On my way out to meet them on the main road," Chance confirmed.

"Then get him out of my sight." Brax turned to Hawkins. He needed to keep the man from killing Robert right now. "Just do me a favor? Call it what I'm owed for giving you what you want."

"What is it?"

"Get him far from here before you do what you plan to do. He's still close enough to San Antonio that there could be blowback on me just because we're related. I'm trying to run a business, you know?"

It was a risk, but Hawkins appeared to appreciate this. "Fair enough. I'll get him far enough from here that the blowback won't fall on you. Seems he made your life difficult enough already."

"Don't get me started." Brax removed his earpiece when neither of the other men were looking and glanced down at the empty car seat.

Was this all that was left of his life? An empty car seat? The memory of what had brought him indescribable happiness and contentment? Even if it was, Tessa and Walker would be together and safe. The way it was meant to be. He could take that with him wherever he went.

His family would be safe. Brax might be alone, but they would be safe.

"Who are you?"

His head snapped up at Hawkins's question.

And everything turned upside down.

"Wow," Prince Riviera chuckled as he dragged a gagged Tessa into the warehouse with a pistol to her head. "I thought you were supposed to be a good guy, Patterson. But you just sold your brother out even though you know he's gonna end up dead."

Chapter Twenty-Five

Tessa had no idea what had happened.

One minute she was hurrying to her car, glad everything had gone okay and Hawkins had let her go so easily. Imagining being reunited with her son, living with him. No fear. Nobody to keep them apart anymore. She could be his mother openly.

Then, while she'd been waiting in the car for Brax or one of the others to come for her like they'd promised, the door had opened. She'd screamed as Prince Riviera had reached in and pulled her out by her hair.

Not that she'd ever had the displeasure of meeting him before then—she'd recognized Riviera from the news. Tall, thin, with a mouth that was curled up in a permanent sneer. Like he knew something the rest of the world didn't.

She would've screamed again to signal Brax, but Prince had a gun, which was the only thing that could have silenced her. He'd pressed it to her temple with a laugh, and one glimpse of his dark, empty eyes had chilled her to the bone.

"I don't know what the hell's going on here,"

he'd whispered, holding her close, "but you and I are going inside to have a little talk with Patterson."

He'd then shoved her back into the car, sitting her sideways so her feet were on the ground, his gun still at her head while the friend he'd brought with him went over to the warehouse to listen in. He'd come back, reporting what had gone down.

Prince had laughed softly, shaking his head. "Maybe we were coming at this Brax the wrong way. I didn't think he had it in him to do something like that."

Then, holding her arm in a painful grip that had hurt as much as the patch of scalp he'd pulled her hair from, he had dragged her to the warehouse. "Come on," he'd snorted. "Let's go in and have a talk with your boyfriend."

Just when she'd convinced herself a future with Brax was possible, probable—maybe even certain—the gun at her head had turned her insides to water.

All she could do as Prince had pulled her into the warehouse was thank the heavens that Walker wasn't there. That he was safe.

She couldn't say the same for herself.

IT WAS BRAX'S worst nightmare come true.

Not because he'd had any fear for himself. It didn't matter what happened to him, not now. But Tessa… he couldn't live if anything happened to her. And right then, with her mouth gagged and a gun to her head? A gun held by none other than Prince Riviera?

A beyond-worst nightmare come true.

"What's this all about?" Hawkins demanded. "What do you think you're doing?"

"Shut up," Riviera spat. "I'm talking to my friend over here, Mr. Patterson. He's a tough man to get a hold of, you know? I've been looking for him ever since my friends paid him a visit a few days ago."

"Yeah, thanks for that." Brax's gaze moved to Tessa, whose eyes were wide enough to bulge. "Did you hurt her?"

"Nothing she won't recover from given enough time," Riviera sneered. "Don't worry about it. You wouldn't want to waste your final moments worrying, would you?"

"Just…just lower the gun, okay? You want to talk? You want to work something out?" Brax took one tentative step toward them. Then another. "Fine. We can talk this out. But I can't concentrate if she has a gun shoved in her face. That's just how it is."

"Like I care what you want or don't want." Riviera's laughter was cold, empty, just like his eyes and his smile. He reminded Brax of a shark.

A shark that smelled blood. He could probably sense Brax's barely concealed panic.

Except a shark didn't toy with its prey. It didn't take any pleasure from watching people squirm.

"Lower the gun, and we can work this out. She hasn't done anything. She's no threat to you." Another tentative step. Another.

Riviera pulled Tessa closer to him. Bile rose in Brax's throat at the thought of that monster touching her. Hurting her. There was pain in her eyes, no doubt from the way Riviera's fingers dug into her arm.

"Okay. Fine. Talk to me." He lowered the gun, letting his arm hang at his side. "What do you have to say?"

"I'll back out of testifying," Brax offered. "No worries. You can have your little cartel to yourself and continue doing whatever it is you do without having to concern yourself with me."

Riviera looked him up and down. "Really? Just like that? This was all I had to do, huh?" He laughed softly, looking at Tessa. "Your boyfriend isn't so hard to get along with as long as a guy knows where his soft spots are. And he's obviously got a huge soft spot for you, cutie."

Brax bit his tongue.

If only he could hear Weston or Chance in his ear, but he'd already taken the earpiece out. Putting it back in now would give away the entire plan. Hawkins and Robert were behind him, both of them silent. Probably frozen in shock.

"Would it make you feel better if I told you I want money to keep quiet?" Brax asked with a shrug. Anything to stall. The best he could hope for right now was for one of his brothers to hear what was happening and call in backup.

But what if they weren't listening anymore? What if they were waiting for Hawkins, unaware of what was going on here?

Riviera smirked. "Now you're speaking my language, Brax. Money. That's what lies at the heart of everything, doesn't it? My man outside overheard you talking about money in here. Your, uh, what is it? Brother? Your brother can't give the people he owes what he owes them if he's dead."

"That's right," Brax said, thankful that for once Robert knew enough to keep his mouth shut.

"That's an astute observation on your part. That's the kind of thinking an intelligent man does. You can't get your money from someone if he's dead."

Riviera looked at Tessa, a nasty smile tugging at the corner of his mouth. "Then again, why would a smart man bother giving somebody money when he could just kill him and get it over with?"

Brax's insides went cold when Riviera raised the gun again and pointed it at Tessa. "But I'll take care of you first, cutie, since I've learned an important lesson. Never leave a witness alive."

There was no time to think about it, no time to try to get Riviera to listen to reason. There was no reasoning with a monster—something without feelings, without morals—anyway. He was going to kill Tessa. This was not a man who made idle threats. He wouldn't think twice about killing an innocent woman in cold blood.

There was no backup and nobody to help him. He'd be taking a bullet.

But if there was one thing Brax knew with complete certainty, it was that life without Tessa wasn't worth living. He had no desire to even try it. Even the idea of going off the grid and being without her was unthinkable. He doubted now, in this moment of clarity, that he would ever have managed it.

Which was why he threw himself at Prince Riviera, gun and all. If he got shot, he got shot.

As long as *she* didn't.

A shot rang out. Brax hit the floor with Riviera under him, bouncing the crime boss's head off the concrete, knocking him unconscious.

He waited for the pain from the bullet to set in, but there was no pain. Why wasn't there pain? There'd been a shot. Everything had happened too fast.

He looked up at Tessa, who was still standing. No blood. Just a lot of fear.

"Brax! Report!" Weston's frantic voice coming from outside.

"All clear!" he managed. He stumbled to his feet and rushed to Tessa.

She fell against him as he worked the gag from her mouth. He took her face into his hands and looked her over. "Are you okay?"

"I'm okay. I'm okay." But she jumped when Weston rushed into the warehouse with his gun drawn.

"He had a friend with him," Weston reported. "He had a bead on you from outside the building. I took care of him." Seconds later, red and blue flashing lights flooded through the windows and the open door.

So that was where the shot had come from. It had been his brother saving his life.

Brax could only wrap his arms around Tessa,

wanting to pull her inside of him and keep her there forever.

"You're safe now," he whispered into her ear as she trembled. "You're safe. It's all okay."

"You could've gotten yourself killed!" She glared up at him. "Don't you know that? What would've happened if you had ended up dead?"

"I didn't care about staying alive as long as you had a chance to get away."

Her eyes welled up with fresh tears. "Don't say that. Don't say you were willing to die for me."

"What if it's the truth?" He tucked her hair behind her ear, letting his fingers linger against her smooth jaw, her throat, her cheek. "I knew when you were standing there with that gun to your head that I wasn't interested in living if it meant being without you. Because I love you."

"Yeah?" In spite of the tears now pouring down her cheeks, she smiled.

"Oh, yeah," he whispered. "I love you, Tessa Mahoney. And I would face a hundred armed gunmen for your sake. You and Walker are my entire world. You're all I want. All I'll ever need."

He caught her lips in the sweetest, most tender kiss. As precious as she'd been to him before then, having almost lost her only made every moment she was in his arms more meaningful.

"I love you so much," she beamed before falling against him, her wet cheek on his chest. He held her, stroking her hair, watching as Robert, Hawkins and Prince Riviera were led away in zip ties.

"You managed to get Riviera's confession too." Weston grinned, striding over to them. "Talking all about how he planned to kill a witness. You don't need to testify now, brother. I'd call that a solid day's work."

Brax could only laugh. "Yeah. A solid day's work."

Chapter Twenty-Six

"Let me help you with that." Tessa handed Walker off to Brax before hurrying to help Sheila with the food she was taking from the oven.

"You've gone to so much trouble." Claire marveled, looking over the spread Brax's mother had prepared.

"It's no trouble, fixing my boys' favorite dishes." Sheila beamed as she looked over the full kitchen. "Having everybody here at once is more than enough reason to celebrate. But today is important. Worthy of a feast."

Tessa grinned over at Brax, who lifted Walker's hand in a wave.

"That's right, pal," he murmured. "You and Mama are going to be together for always now."

"It only took four weeks." Clinton shook his head as he entered the room. "Let it never be said the wheels of justice turn quickly."

"We know all about that," Sheila reminded him. "Not so much the justice bit, but waiting for red tape to be cleared. We went through it four times, remember?"

Clinton slid an arm around his wife and kissed the top of her head.

Brax marveled, and not for the first time, at how lucky he'd been. He had a couple of parents who'd always been an example of a loving partnership. One based on mutual respect, friendship, and affection.

Claire paused in the middle of putting together a fruit salad. "How does it feel now that the judge has restored your parental rights?"

"Like I've been given the whole world." Tessa glowed. She might as well have floated above the floor she was so overjoyed.

Brax knew how she felt. He'd felt that way once he was certain that she was safe, that there was nothing and no one who could hurt her anymore.

Knowing she had full custody again brought him deep satisfaction too. This was how it should be.

"Game's on," Luke announced before rummaging through the fridge for a drink.

"That's all you have to say when we're in here toiling away for you?" Claire clicked her tongue and shook her head.

"Hey, I never claimed to be great in the kitchen. My announcement of the game being on was my contribution. That and, well, eating." He leaned in and kissed Claire's cheek. She only laughed and shook her head again.

"Here, you can contribute this way." Brax handed Walker over to his brother and did what he could not to laugh at the look of panic on Luke's face.

He wasn't successful. "I didn't hand you a bomb," he snickered. "Take it easy."

"I have to say—" Sheila dropped a broad wink in Claire's direction "—you look good holding a baby, son."

Tessa met Brax's gaze, and they both grinned. It was almost too obvious the way Sheila hinted heavily at Claire and Luke giving her grandkids.

Luke's face went red. "Good thing there's a baby around to hold." Though he wasn't fooling anybody. The way he looked at Walker, who waved his fists and babbled happily, told the real story.

Chance and Weston set the table as per their mom's orders. Clinton pulled one casserole dish after another out of the oven while Sheila fretted over whether they had enough wine. Tessa put the finishing touches on a pan of macaroni and cheese, sprinkling buttered breadcrumbs on top. Claire and Luke fussed over Walker.

Brax had never felt happier and more at peace in his life.

Which was why what he planned to do that special day was the easiest move he'd ever considered. There wasn't a scrap of doubt in his mind.

Tessa was his home. She was just as much his family as the rest of the people around them.

The tricky part was how to do it.

After serving themselves from the array of dishes and platters on the counter, they gathered around the table.

"It's all delicious." Tessa marveled. "I love to cook, but I don't think I've ever cooked this much food at once. How do you manage?"

"It's practice." Sheila shrugged. "I had to feed four growing boys at once, not to mention a husband with a healthy appetite."

"If you didn't cook so well, I wouldn't want seconds all the time," Clinton pointed out.

"Seconds? Try thirds, Clinton Patterson."

"Whatever magic you work, I would love to learn some of your recipes. Like this mac and cheese." Tessa let out a soft groan as she took a bite.

"I guess if you're going to spend time with my Brax, you'd better learn how to cook my recipes." Sheila gave Brax a very knowing, very motherly look.

He made a mental note to ask just how she managed to read their minds the way she did. There was no keeping secrets from the woman.

Tessa fed Walker mashed bananas, which was a fairly new development and needed her complete attention or else everything in a three-foot radius would end up covered in Walker's snack.

It was now or never, he realized. This was the moment. With his family together, laughing, happy. With Tessa secure, knowing no one could take her son away. With everyone who had tried to hurt the ones he loved behind bars, Brax's life had never been more perfect.

Which was why he slid the box from his pocket while Tessa's back was turned. He opened it then placed it on the table where she couldn't help but see it when she turned away from Walker.

Claire clamped a hand over her mouth.

Sheila held her hands up, signaling for silence. She didn't need to, since everyone went quiet once they realized what was going on.

Finally, Tessa noticed. "Is everything okay?" she asked in a panicked tone.

Then she saw the box and the ring inside.

"Oh, my goodness." She looked at Brax. "What is this?"

"What do you think it is?" he asked, more nervous than he'd ever been in his entire life. Why was he shaking?

"Brax…oh, my goodness." She crossed her hands over her chest as tears started to flow.

"You know by now that I love you," he murmured, "and that you and Walker are my world. I want us to be a real family. I want you to be my wife. I want Walker to be my son. You'd make me the happiest man who ever drew breath if you would agree to marry me."

"Agree?" She burst out laughing. "Like there was any doubt?"

"That's a yes?" he asked, still tentative.

"Of course, it is!" She nearly knocked him off his chair when she threw her arms around his neck and squeezed until he could hardly breathe.

But that was just fine. He could take it.

"Oh, it's about time!" Sheila crowed, laughing and crying and clapping.

"About time?" Chance laughed. "It hasn't been all that long that they've been together."

"Sweetheart, if there's one thing I've learned, it's

this—when you know, you know. And I knew the minute that woman stepped foot in this house that she was right for my Brax."

"See?" Brax whispered in Tessa's ear. "Mom knew. I guess that means we're both on the right track. She's never wrong."

Tessa loosened her grip on him enough to pull back with an ear-to-ear smile. "Then I guess she has more to teach me than recipes."

"Nah. You're pretty perfect just the way you are." He pulled the ring from the box and slid it over her finger. Everyone in the room broke out in cheers and applause.

Even Walker raised his tiny fists and shouted.

Brax and Tessa leaned against each other and laughed. "He approves," Tessa noted. "We're definitely on the right track."

* * * * *

Look for the next book in USA TODAY
*bestselling author Janie Crouch's
miniseries, San Antonio Security,
when* Texas Bodyguard: Weston
goes on sale next month.

*And in case you missed it,
Luke's story is available now,
wherever Harlequin Intrigue books are sold!*

#2139 RIDING SHOTGUN
The Cowboys of Cider Creek • by Barb Han
Family secrets collide when Emmerson Bennett's search for her birth mother exposes her to the Hayes's cattle ranching dynasty. But Rory Hayes's honor won't allow him to abandon the vulnerable stranger, even when she puts him and his family in the line of fire...

#2140 CASING THE COPYCAT
Covert Cowboy Soldiers • by Nicole Helm
Rancher Dunne Thompson spent his adult life trying to atone for his serial killer grandfather. But redemption comes in the form of mysterious Quinn Peterson and her offer to help him catch a copycat murderer. They make an unexpected and perfect team...until the deadly culprit targets them both.

#2141 OVER HER DEAD BODY
Defenders of Battle Mountain • by Nichole Severn
Targeted by a shooter, single mom Isla Vachs and her daughter are saved by the man responsible for her husband's death. Adan Sergeant's vow of duty won't be shaken by her resentment. But falling for his best friend's widow could be deadly...or the only way they get out alive.

#2142 WYOMING MOUNTAIN HOSTAGE
Cowboy State Lawmen • by Juno Rushdan
Within moments of revealing her pregnancy to her coworker with benefits, FBI Special Agent Becca Hammond is taken hostage. Agent Jake Delgado won't compromise his partner's life—or their unborn child. But will he risk an entire town's safety just to keep them safe?

#2143 OZARKS MISSING PERSON
Arkansas Special Agents • by Maggie Wells
Attorney Matthew Murray's younger sister is missing and Special Agent Grace Reed is determined to find her. But when the case looks more like murder, both are drawn into a web of power and deceit...and dangerous attraction.

#2144 CRIME SCENE CONNECTION
by Janice Kay Johnson
Journalist Alexa Adams is determined to expose every bad cop in the city. But when danger soon follows, she's forced to trust Lieutenant Matthew Reinert. A man in blue. The enemy. And the only one willing to risk everything to keep her—and her mission—safe from those determined to silence her.

HICNM0323

HARLEQUIN
PLUS

Try the best multimedia subscription service for romance readers like you!

Read, Watch and Play.

Experience the easiest way to get the romance content you crave.

Start your **FREE TRIAL** at
www.harlequinplus.com/freetrial.